THE SILENT WOMAN

OTHER TITLES BY MINKA KENT

The Memory Watcher

The Perfect Roommate

The Thinnest Air

The Silent Woman

The Stillwater Girls

You Have to Believe Me

The Trophy Wife

When I Was You

The Watcher Girl

Unmissing

Gone Again

Dangerous Strangers Thrillers

Imaginary Strangers

THE SILENT WOMAN

A THRILLER

MINKA KENT

This is a work of fiction. Names, characters, organizations, places, events, and incidents are either products of the author's imagination or are used fictitiously. Otherwise, any resemblance to actual persons, living or dead, is purely coincidental.

Text copyright © 2022, 2025 by Nom de Plume, LLC
All rights reserved.

No part of this book may be reproduced, or stored in a retrieval system, or transmitted in any form or by any means, electronic, mechanical, photocopying, recording, or otherwise, without express written permission of the publisher.

Published by Thomas & Mercer, Seattle

www.apub.com

Amazon, the Amazon logo, and Thomas & Mercer are trademarks of Amazon.com, Inc., or its affiliates.

EU product safety contact:
Amazon Media EU S. à r.l.
38, avenue John F. Kennedy, L-1855 Luxembourg
amazonpublishing-gpsr@amazon.com

ISBN-13: 9781662531620 (paperback)
ISBN-13: 9781662531613 (digital)

Cover design by Jarrod Taylor
Cover image: © ZenShui/Milena Boniek, © Prasit photo / Getty;
© New Africa / Shutterstock; © RelaxImages/STUDD / Plainpicture

Printed in the United States of America

For the incomparable Valery Walton.

Listen to silence. It has so much to say.

—Rumi

PART I
PRESENT DAY

1

JADE

I fan to the end of my drugstore paperback and read the last page first.

Surprises have never been my thing. I'm here for the journey, every last titillating paragraph of it, but I need to know how it's going to end first.

My phone vibrates, pattering against my mug of steaming Earl Grey. I set my novel aside and press the green button before placing my husband's call on speakerphone.

"Good morning." I reach for my tea. Taking a careful sip, I gaze beyond the fresh arrangement of Casa Blanca lilies anchoring the kitchen table, toward the leafy backyard with its sparkling Spanish-tiled pool. And then I settle my attention on the picturesque caretaker's cottage—where Wells's first wife resides.

"About to present. Just wanted to hear your voice before I head in." His words are breathier than usual. He's never been one to let anyone see him sweat, but presenting a home he's been designing for an entire year to a demanding client would be nerve-racking for the most stoic of individuals. "Wish me luck."

"Luck is the last thing you need," I say, wearing the same playful grin that always finds its way to my lips whenever I hear his voice. "You've got this."

"Did you get the flowers?"

"All seven of them," I say. "Thank you."

Rising from my chair, I lean closer to the small bouquet and drag the enchanting smell of Casa Blanca lilies into my lungs. Wells had them delivered this morning, along with a note indicating the seven flowers represented the seven days he'll be away and missing me.

He's always been a details man.

Over the next week, he'll be in Charleston, meeting with his client and his client's builder and interior designer. At fifteen thousand square feet and five acres of wooded land, it's his biggest residential project to date. The renderings he's shown me are breathtaking—French-inspired domes, marble fireplaces, and a sweeping double staircase in the two-story entrance. I can only imagine how it'll turn out in real life.

"All right," he says. "They're here. I've got to go. I'll call you the second I'm back at my hotel tonight. I love you."

"I love you, too." The words are still foreign on my tongue. I've never been one to fall head over heels that easily, and growing up, we weren't a family who said that word very often. If we did, it was almost always written in a card and intentionally misspelled, like *luv u bunches*, a simple *xo*, or a hastily scribbled heart.

But I say it because I mean it, and I say it for him. That's what marriage is about—growing as a person, making your partner happy, and sometimes that requires getting out of your comfort zone.

Heading to the sink to rinse my mug, I peer into the backyard again, my gaze fixed on the guesthouse where my silent predecessor resides.

Wells told me he and Sylvie were trying to have a baby before her unfortunate accident, that she wanted nothing more in this world than to be a mother, that they'd been trying fruitlessly for a while and were about to make an appointment with a specialist to see what was going on. She was so excited, so full of hope, so ready, he told me.

Fate can be cruel.

And then it can be crueler still.

Before we married last month, Wells warned me that our arrangement would be unconventional—delicate—but when you love someone, you accept their baggage just as they accept yours.

I check my watch and take a deep breath. I've got a call in twenty minutes with my agent. She emailed me yesterday, asking if I had a few minutes to "touch base." I'm certain she thinks I'm taking my sweet time with my current manuscript. And maybe I am. But only because I'm enjoying the process so much the idea of finishing it fills me with dread.

A year ago, who'd have thought I'd land a seven-figure contract to write the first and only authorized biography on the late and enigmatic golden-age Hollywood icon Viviette Westmore? Who'd have thought I'd be married to her one and only grandson? That I'd be living in her historic Brentwood estate, one filled with all of her personal effects and untouched by time?

Most mornings I could pinch myself.

This time last year, I was holed up in a shoebox apartment, subsisting off ramen and Folgers, quelling my loneliness with laughably bad Tinder dates. My student loans were in their final month of forbearance and my ancient Hyundai was one scorching summer day from overheating on the 405 again.

The day I met Wells changed the course of my life forever.

I'm about to head upstairs to work when a blur of movement outside the window captures my attention. I glance outside to find Sylvie's day nurse sprinting from the cottage to the pool before trotting toward the back door by the kitchen. With her oversized purse clutched tight against her side, she pounds on the windowpane portion of the door, her palm flat and her eyes wide.

My stomach drops.

"Hello?" she calls before knocking again, her voice sharp against the glass. "Is anyone home?"

I can't get to her fast enough, unfastening the latch and yanking on the stuck door with all of my might.

"Hi . . . what's going on?" I ask, realizing I haven't the slightest idea what her name is.

I don't know any of Sylvie's nurses' or caretakers' names; Wells handles all of that.

She exhales, lifting a trembling hand to her chest. "Thank goodness someone's home. I have a family emergency, and I need to go. I've called the supervising nurse and left a message. I just wanted someone to know Sylvie's by herself right now . . ."

"Have you called Wells?" I ask, though I'm not sure why it would make a difference. He's in meetings all day. There's nothing he can do from two thousand miles away.

"Yes, ma'am," she says before checking her watch. Her name badge is crooked, but I manage to catch her name: *Eliza*. "Mr. Westmore didn't answer. I have to leave—I'm so sorry. Sylvie still needs to take her morning pills, but she can't take them on an empty stomach. I'm not sure when they'll send someone else to cover, but I . . ."

Eliza's words fade into nothing as our eyes hold for a moment that feels longer than it is.

She doesn't have to finish her thought. I already know what she's asking. And the look in her focused gaze tells me she's fully aware of Wells's wish that no one enter the cottage besides nurses—and him.

With her fragile state of mind and inability to communicate, no one is sure what all Sylvie is able to comprehend. Wells has made it abundantly clear that he doesn't want to cause her undue stress nor does he want to burden me with managing her care. I've assured him many times that her care would never burden me, but from what I understand, her condition is complex. She's a riddle even the finest doctors in the world have yet to solve.

"I'll handle it," I say, offering a reassuring smile to hide the icy blanket of panic washing over me. "Go ahead. I've got this."

I inject confidence in my words despite it not belonging there.

It's me . . . or no one.

"Her pills are on the counter," Eliza says. "The instructions are on the bottles. She likes brown sugar oatmeal for breakfast. Scrambled eggs with butter. No salt or pepper."

"Got it."

"Coffee is okay, but no orange juice," she adds, walking backward with uneven strides. "The vitamin C interferes with the absorption of one of her meds."

I nod, sliding my trembling hands in my back pockets. "Understood."

"She needs to take her pills in the next half hour. Any later and she won't sleep tonight."

I overheard Wells talking on the phone with Sylvie's doctors once, and while I wasn't trying to listen in, I couldn't mistake a handful of words that stuck out clear as day: *manic, catatonic, physical outbursts, lethargic, unstable, mood stabilizers, appetite stimulants* . . .

I got the sense that they were simply layering medications on top of each other in an attempt to cancel out unwanted side effects. But I didn't want to pry. It wasn't my place, and it's none of my business.

Eliza nearly trips over a terra-cotta flowerpot on her way, but in an instant, she's out of sight. Lingering in the open doorway, I steer my attention to the cottage and swallow the lump building in my throat.

Three years ago, Wells found Sylvie face down in the pool, blood gushing from the side of her head. He managed to pull her out, call 9-1-1, and begin CPR as she wasn't breathing.

He saved her life.

But her life was never the same after that.

Closing the back door, I pace the kitchen before stopping at the island to collect myself.

Aside from the occasional flutter of a sheer curtain or lithe shadow moving behind a darkened window, I've only seen Sylvie Westmore in photographs.

I shut my eyes, draw in a long, slow breath, and convince myself that helping her is the right thing to do, that no matter what happens, Wells will understand. He'll be grateful, I'm sure.

The trill of my phone sends a start to my chest. I suck in a sharp breath and wait for my heart rate to settle as my agent's name flashes across the screen.

In the midst of all of this, I'd spaced on our call.

"Julie, hi. I'm so sorry," I answer. "I'm going to have to reschedule."

"Everything all right?" She hardly disguises the annoyance in her tone. Not that I blame her. My publisher is breathing down her neck; therefore, she needs to breathe down mine. That's how this works. Pressure creates diamonds, and this diamond of a biography needs to be flawless.

"No, um, something just came up," I say, thinking fast. "A bit of a . . . family emergency."

Wells is my family, Sylvie was his, it's the only way I can describe this without going into detail or inviting questions I'm not prepared to answer.

"My God, Jade. I'm so sorry. Anything I can do?" she asks from her high-rise office in Manhattan.

"Thank you," I say, "but I'm handling it. I'll call you this afternoon?"

"Of course. I'll be here."

I end the call and wipe my sweaty palms on the sides of my thighs as prickles of sweat collect across my brow.

Plucking the Casa Blanca lilies from the table, I carry them to the sink, trim the stems, and place them in a small, fluted glass vase—one that once belonged to Viviette. They say it's in poor taste to show up to someone's home for the first time empty-handed, but this will have to do on such short notice. I'm not sure what she's able to understand, but I don't want to assume she's nothing more than a living, breathing bag of bones.

Palms fastened carefully around the crystal jar, I begin to make my way to the cottage with my heart in my teeth every step of the way.

I have approximately thirty seconds to prepare what I'm going to say to Sylvie, though it's impossible to know if she'll understand any of it. Maybe it's just a vain attempt to make myself feel better about this whole arrangement, to relieve myself of the guilt that gnaws away at me little by little every time I look back at the cottage.

My beautiful, charmed little life is a direct result of someone else's personal tragedy—the heaviness of that painful fact is not lost on me.

In an instant I'm standing at her door, my feet anchored onto the small cement pad, no recollection of the trek here.

I rap lightly against the door and listen for footsteps. I don't want to barge in. Then again, it's what everyone else does. The day nurse, the night nurse, the laundress, the grocery delivery service, Wells . . .

Squinting into the window, I spot her thin frame sitting in a plush recliner the color of gray skies. Her unblinking stare is fixed on the flickering TV on the other side of the room. Her hands rest on the tops of her blanket-covered thighs, balled into loose fists. If it weren't for the slow, subtle rise and fall of her chest, there'd be no way to know she's alive.

I knock again, just in case.

But Sylvie doesn't move.

Securing the vase under one arm, I twist the doorknob and step inside.

"Sylvie?" I say. "Hi. I'm Jade."

2

JADE

"I brought you flowers." I hold out the stark-white blossoms with their deep red stamens. "Casa Blanca lilies."

Two chatty middle-aged women from a syndicated talk show fill the silence between us. Sylvie has yet to acknowledge me—though perhaps she isn't able to. She's yet to blink either.

"Your nurse had to take off," I say, "so I came to make you breakfast."

I speak slowly, my voice tipping a little louder than usual. Clearing my throat, I remind myself she isn't deaf or hard of hearing.

"I don't know if you heard me when I first came in." I take a step closer, clutching the vase in both hands. I'd place it on the coffee table beside her, but it's already covered in various items: a hospital water jug, crumpled Kleenex, a TV remote, and a bottle of unscented Vaseline lotion. It's a far cry from the glamorous life she led before. "My name is Jade."

I offer a warm smile and will her to look at me.

She doesn't.

She simply sits there unmoving, her mousy-brown hair tucked behind her ears and her feet shoved into floral-covered, sherpa-lined house slippers better suited for someone twice her age.

I debate whether to introduce myself as Wells's wife before opting against it. I'm not sure what he's told her about me yet, and I don't want to muddy those waters without consulting him first. It's not my place.

A commercial for some class-action mesothelioma lawsuit fills the screen, the volume ratcheting up a handful of notches as it tends to do whenever an ad comes on. Without thinking, I swipe the remote off the table beside her and tap the volume button lower. Only before I can finish, a bony hand wraps around my wrist—as if to tell me to stop.

Her eyes—as deep and ambiguously dark as a moonlit horizon—burn into mine.

I gasp before tamping down my fright in case it's emanating off me in waves. I don't want to offend her, even if she caught me off guard, even if she can't grasp what's going on.

"I'm so sorry." I release my hold on the remote and she releases her hold on me. She doesn't nod or blink, but the tension leaving her rigid posture makes me think she might understand. "Your nurse said you like oatmeal for breakfast? And scrambled eggs?"

Sylvie's eyes, with their downy lashes the color of milk chocolate, search mine. In the photos I've seen of her from her heyday, she was a knockout. A vivacious brunette with hourglass curves and a contagious mile-wide smile. But her natural beauty wasn't filled, plumped, or lasered. She wore her laugh lines with pride and never shied away from flaunting her figure in a bikini despite it being less than an "LA 10."

Not only that, but she founded a not-for-profit organization that paired senior dogs with senior citizens . . . on top of volunteering as a Big Sister and meeting with a local group to clean beaches the first Sunday of every month. I got the sense she had a bona fide saint complex, though Wells has never mentioned anything about her past. Google searches have been fruitless for the most part. Nothing but a handful of images from local nightlife magazines and a couple of heartfelt articles about her canine companion charity.

Wells once told me he proposed to her six times before she finally said yes—which was why they married on the sixth of June that year.

It isn't hard to see why he fell for her back then.

By all accounts, she was the ultimate catch.

When Wells and I first started dating, I did some online sleuthing on him—as one does in the beginnings of any romantic relationship these days. Aside from some random magazine interviews about his grandmother and a fair amount of red carpet charity photos, there wasn't much to unearth. But I managed to find a dozen or so videos from their wedding eight years ago—each of them simply hashtagged *#WellsAndSylvieForever* on Instagram.

From what I gathered, their memorable night was hosted on these very premises under a blanket of Southern California stars, catered by some celebrity chef flown in from Rome, and attended by a star-studded guest list that would make most people in this city absinthe green with envy.

The catatonic woman sitting before me couldn't possibly be the buxom bride in the tulle Marchesa wedding gown with the plunging neckline, the one stealing kisses from her handsome new husband before dragging him onto the dance floor.

And yet it is.

"I'll be in the kitchen if you need anything," I point across the room toward a space that passes for more of a studio apartment kitchenette than a kitchen. With its small fridge, compact electric oven, countertop microwave, hotel-room-sized coffee maker, and row of cabinets, I suppose it covers all the bases. But it's nothing compared to the setup in the main house. According to Wells, it's the only part of his grandmother's house he remodeled, and only out of necessity and safety. He even went so far as to hire professionals to carefully remove, package, and store all of the original pieces in a climate-controlled storage unit should he ever want to restore the kitchen to its original glory.

Someday, he plans to make Westhaven—the name with which Viviette christened the estate—into a museum akin to Graceland or Hearst Castle, Pickfair before it was razed.

Until then, it's his home.

Our home.

I place the vase of lilies on the counter next to the sink and help myself to the fridge, pulling out eggs and butter before locating a box of brown sugar oatmeal in the cupboard. Next, I find a frying pan and a ceramic bowl and get to work.

While the eggs cook over low heat, I scour the small space for coffee grounds and pray I don't mess this part up. I've never been a coffee drinker. The last time I made a pot, I was twelve and it was Mother's Day. The resulting liquid was as thick as sludge and blacker than black, but my mom sipped it with a smile.

I come across a package of organic decaf blond roast in the cupboard by the range, spinning it around to look for instructions and breathing a sigh of relief when I find them.

I'm plating Sylvie's food a few minutes later when a row of pill bottles catch my eye. There must be at least eight of them, if not more.

I put her breakfast aside and examine the orange-brown bottles, each one topped with a childproof lock and various orange and yellow stickers with bold pharmaceutical warnings: *take with food, do not operate heavy machinery while taking this medication, may cause drowsiness, do not take with dairy, may affect iron absorption, may cause loss of appetite* . . .

Studying the labels and instructions, I determine five of them are to be taken after breakfast. I slide them away from the others, grab Sylvie's plate, and turn to carry it to the two-person bistro table by the window—only the moment I spin on my heel, I'm met with Sylvie standing in the middle of the kitchen, a few feet from me.

I hadn't heard her get up.

I didn't know she *could* get up . . .

My heart hammers in my chest, but I manage a pleasant smile.

"I'll set you up over here." I nod toward the table and rest her plate on a jute place mat. "Still need to pour your coffee."

Without a word, she makes her way to the table in her sherpa-lined slippers, takes a seat, and stares out the window—one with a direct view to the kitchen and breakfast nook in the main house.

For her sake, I hope she doesn't understand any of what's going on. I hope she's a blank slate, without a single thought behind her eyes.

It would kill me to think she was sitting in this little cottage with all of her keepers, witnessing someone else live the life she should still be living.

I pour her coffee, contemplating whether or not I should ask how she takes it, but there's no point if she can't answer me. I give it to her black. She takes a sip and doesn't grimace.

Helping myself to the seat across from her, I figure I ought to supervise, or at the very least, be on standby should she need something. I imagine that's what her nurses do. Knowing Wells, he wouldn't tolerate anything less than their full attention at all times.

With slow and steady movements, she forks bits of pale yellow egg and lifts it to her mouth. Her lips are slightly chapped, their color the palest of pinks. The TV blares from the other side of the room and the petite fridge in the kitchenette hums.

Other than that and the two of us, there's no other sign of life.

"I should get your medications." I scoot out from the table and make my way to the kitchen counter, retrieving one pill from each of the five bottles along with a glass of water. I place them all next to her mug of coffee. "Whenever you're finished eating, of course."

Her midnight-blue stare flicks to mine as she chews.

I relieve myself from her heavy gaze and peer around the cozy space we're sharing. On the far side of the room is an open door, one that offers a glimpse of her bedroom. Her bed is unmade, the duvet half hanging off the mattress, pooling on the floor. I know housekeeping comes every Monday and Thursday, but it's Tuesday and already this place could use some straightening up.

"Would you like me to make your bed?" I ask.

She slides a spoon into her oatmeal, reacting as if she didn't hear me at all.

It isn't a no, so I take that as a yes.

The distinct scent of hand sanitizer and hospital antiseptic hits me the instant I step foot inside her bedroom, reminiscent of the way it smelled when my grandmother had a stroke the summer I turned fourteen and we visited her at Mercy General every day for weeks. I swear that odor lingered on my skin and hair and the inside of my nostrils for months.

A stack of thick drugstore paperbacks at least five deep rests on her nightstand alongside a book light. Thrillers mostly. Thick, chunky fonts on the covers and ominous titles. James Patterson. Clive Cussler. J. D. Robb. Whether they're hers or the night nurse's, I can't be sure.

Thick velvet curtains the color of sawdust cover the only window on the east wall, and I pull them back to let a little morning sunlight in and take away some of the depressive darkness. After that, I straighten her sheets, followed by the duvet, and I finish by giving the pillows a decent fluffing.

When I'm finished with her bed, I gather a handful of crumpled clothes from a chair in the corner—mostly white cotton nightgowns and satin housecoats in various pastel shades—and place them in a wicker hamper next to her dresser . . . which houses a myriad of framed photos.

Upon closer inspection, I discover each and every one of them is of Sylvie and Wells.

The largest of them, an eight-by-ten candid photo from their wedding day. Tightness stretches across my chest and my eyes prick with damp tears that I blink away before they have a chance to fall.

The image is in black and white, the bride and groom sporting carefree smiles as their moment is locked into a single timeless photograph.

My heart aches for Wells.

For Sylvie.

For what they once had.

For what they'll never have again.

The day after I told my mother Wells and I were engaged, she asked me why I'd ever settle for second place in a man's heart. But I've never seen in that way. It isn't a competition.

Wells and Sylvie's marriage is over. Physically. Emotionally. Legally. A man's needs can't be fulfilled by a woman who can't speak, who can't express her love, who requires around-the-clock care, and who can't function on her own. A woman who can't travel the world with him or listen to him wax poetic on the laurels of his architectural idols, Frank Gehry and I. M. Pei.

Wells could have shipped her to a private care facility and left her to spend the rest of her days out of sight, out of mind.

But he refused.

Instead, he set her up in the caretaker's cottage of his grandmother's property, where he could ensure she would never be out of arm's reach of him; where he could supervise her care firsthand, visit her, ensure she was happy, healthy, and comfortable—all things considered.

Their union was over, but Wells refused to abandon Sylvie.

Wells once told me that he and Sylvie made a pact—should something unspeakable happen to one of them during their marriage, the other had permission to move on, to find joy and happiness however they could. They cared for one another so deeply, they couldn't bear the thought of the other spending the rest of their life alone, lonely, or half fulfilled.

If that isn't love, I don't know what is.

I place the photo back where I found it and return to the kitchen, where Sylvie is swallowing the last of her pills.

Taking the seat across from her once more, I cross my legs and settle in until the replacement nurse arrives.

The TV show in the living room goes to commercial, leaving a few seconds of dead silence that only emphasize the discomfiture of this moment. I wish I could ask her what she knows, what she understands, if she's okay . . .

I can only imagine all the things she'd say if she could.

"I can take these if you're all finished." I gesture to her breakfast dishes.

I'm midreach when her attention focuses on my left ring finger—specifically the cushion-cut garnet with the diamond-and-gold art deco band. It's far from a traditional diamond solitaire, but I wouldn't have it any other way. It once belonged to his grandmother—a gift from some European prince she dated in the sixties. The man was mad for Viviette, showering her with lavish gifts and grand gestures to the point of obsession. She sent every last thing back except for this ring, and she only kept it because her sister hated garnets—and loved the prince.

Viviette and her sister, Babette, had a strange and complicated dynamic, one I'm insatiably digging into as I pen her biography. These are the details I live for, the sort of fascinating tidbits that keep readers turning pages long after midnight.

Without warning, Sylvie wraps her hand around my wrist, pulling the ring close. Her dry lips flatten, and her eyes narrow, as if she's trying to say something. Her bony fingers dig into my flesh so hard my skin flashes white, a move more unsettling than painful.

Jerking my hand back, I massage the tender parts and clutch it against my chest.

She reaches for my hand again, except this time there's a wildness in her expression that wasn't there before. I think back to the conversation I overheard, when Wells mentioned her angry outbursts.

"It was a gift," I say. "From Wells."

Details aren't important. Not here. Not now. Not yet.

Rising from her chair, she slams a balled fist on the table, jolting the glass salt and pepper shakers in the center of the table.

A flash of cold runs through me before settling like an anchor in the pit of my stomach.

This was a bad idea.

Sylvie points at my hand with a spindly, trembling finger.

She clearly recognizes the ring—and the fact that it's on my left ring finger—which means she comprehends more than I thought.

I shouldn't have come here.

I shouldn't have done this.

Though what choice did I have? I couldn't leave her alone.

Wells was right—a change in her routine is too much for her to handle.

There's no denying she's distraught.

I splay my palms in the air as if to somehow convey to her that I'm harmless, that I mean well, that everything's going to be okay.

A flash of something outside catches my eye. I peel my careful gaze from Sylvie in time to spot an older woman in lavender scrubs making her way across our backyard. The replacement nurse couldn't have come at a better time.

"Looks like your new nurse is here." I inch toward the door, each step placing much-needed distance between Sylvie and me.

She shuffles across the kitchen, shoving medicine bottles and miscellaneous papers aside before tearing a sheet of paper off a small notepad. Reaching for a pen emblazoned with a pharmaceutical company's logo, she presses the tip against the wrinkled paper so hard it rips with the first stroke. When she's finished, she turns to face me. I attempt to move, but her unnerving stare pins me in place.

What is she doing?

What is she *thinking*?

A knock at the door jerks me out of my watchful trance.

"Hello," the woman calls from outside with a chipper, sing-song tone. "It's Glenna with Visiting Nurses."

"Come on in," I say as Sylvie hands me the wrinkled scrap of paper. I fold it in two and slip it into my pocket. As far as I know, Sylvie hasn't been able to communicate in any way, shape, or form since her accident. "Hi . . . we were just finishing up breakfast."

The nurse sets her purse and bag on the table by the door before stepping out of her shoes.

"This is my first time here," she says with the jovial pleasantness of a kindergarten teacher or longtime grandmother. Scanning the room, she squints. "There should be a black binder somewhere? It's got all the notes from the previous shift as well as medication protocols."

That would've been helpful half an hour ago . . .

"Oh, wait. I see it," she says, shuffling to the living room and plucking it off the love seat. She fans through the first few sheets, adjusting her wire-frame glasses as she reads. "All right. I've got it from here, Mrs. Westmore."

Sylvie's jaw sets as her icy sapphire blues bore into me all over again.

I'm not sure how Glenna knew I was Wells's wife or if it was simply a lucky guess. Either way, if the cat wasn't out of the bag a moment ago, it's halfway across the country by now.

"Thank you so much," I say. "If you need anything, I'll be in the main house."

"It says here to only call Wells for questions or issues . . ." She points to a note written in bold black Sharpie on the inside flap of the binder. The words are underlined thrice.

I force a breath through my nose, lips flat. "Right."

Her brows knit in understandable confusion.

"He's out of town at the moment," I say. "If you need anything, please let me know."

I can't leave fast enough. Every stride that delivers me closer to the main house is accompanied by the realization that I'm going to have to tell Wells about this—specifically about upsetting Sylvie.

As soon as I'm inside, I retrieve the crumpled paper from my pocket, unfolding Sylvie's note as fast as my juddering fingers allow.

My gaze settles on three letters scrawled in shaky black ink across ripped paper.

Those letters?

R—U—N.

3

JADE

"Wells, hi." I answer my husband's call in the middle of the first ring. I wasn't expecting to hear from him again until tonight. Closing my laptop, I lean back in my desk chair. Attempting to write a single sentence this afternoon has been an arduous task. All I can think about is Sylvie's note and the bizarre morning we shared. I've probably replayed the surreal experience in my head at least a dozen times, and at this point, I'm inclined to believe I dreamed it all. "Everything all right? How'd your meeting go?"

"Just breaking for a meal." His words are ever so breathless and nearly canceled out by the background noise, like he's taking a brisk walk through a crowded space. "So far, so good."

"That's wonderful." I toy with the aquamarine pendant hanging from my neck—one that once belonged to his grandmother.

I've made a habit (with Wells's permission) of wearing an item of hers when I'm writing. Sometimes it's a Pucci headscarf. Other times it's a pair of oversized Dior sunglasses resting on top of my head. I'd love to wear one of her Halston dresses at some point, but her waist was impossibly narrow and the fabric is too old and fragile. Anything I can do to feel closer to my subject, to capture their essence, tends to inspire my writing.

"How's your book coming?" he asks.

"It's coming." I reach for one of Viviette's many ceramic pill boxes, flipping open the lilac-painted lid and running my finger along the golden hinge. "Hey, I was going through the journal collection, and it looks like some are missing? I see numbers one through twenty-three, then there's a number thirty. Any idea where the others are?"

Writers are a strange breed with our little routines and customs. When I wrote the biography on controversial Spanish-American textile heiress Gabriela Cortez DiSanto, I wore her favorite perfume every time I sat down at my computer—the classic and biting Yves Saint Laurent Opium. Once, when writing a profile on a young Hollywood starlet who met an untimely demise in 1947, I worked from the very hotel room where she flung herself off the balcony on a snowy New Year's Eve.

Some people method act.

I method write.

"Huh," he says, pausing. "That's really strange. Have you asked Kathryn? Maybe she moved them when she was cleaning?"

"No . . ." Moving them is one thing. Removing them is something else completely.

"I'll look when I get home," he says. "They're probably in a box in some closet."

"Good, because I'd love to get my hands on them for more content. I have a call with my agent this afternoon," I say. "Not looking forward to telling her it's not even close to halfway done."

I need to tell him about Sylvie.

"So, listen," I say. Heat creeps up my neck, and I clear my throat.

"Oh, before I forget—got a call from Sylvie's nursing agency," he says before I have a chance to elaborate. My stomach drops. Does he already know? "Her day nurse had a personal emergency, so they should be sending someone else out any minute."

I don't tell him he's hours late to this information. I know how easy it is to lose track of time when you're preoccupied and out of your element, and he's been preoccupied and out of his element all day.

"I hate to cut this short," he continues, "but I've got to grab a bite and get back in there. We're poring over this thing square inch by square inch."

"Of course, no worries." I inject a smile into my tone despite the fact that the opportunity to come clean is slipping between my fingers. I've never lied to Wells about anything, and while this is more of an omission than a lie, it feels wrong to keep it from him.

"I'll call you tonight when I'm back at the hotel," he says. "And Jade?"

"Yes?"

"I love you."

"I love you, too." I wait for him to hang up first, and then I place my phone screen-side down on the corner of my desk—next to the wrinkled note from Sylvie.

I trace my fingers over her wilted scribble.

Run . . .

Her?

Or me?

From whom?

And why?

Tucking the note in my pocket, I grab my laptop and head down the hall to Viviette's suite in search of more inspiration for today's writing session. I need a change of scenery. An immersive distraction.

Stepping through the monogrammed double doors at the top of the east stairs, I trek across the plush ivory carpet and take a seat at her vanity, a baby-pink piece with crystal knobs and a Venetian marble top thick with gold veins. On the left are what remains of Viviette's skin care products—all of them untouched and unopened for the past twenty years, just as she left them the day she died.

A jar of Pond's Cold Cream rests between a tube of Elizabeth Arden's Eight Hour cream and a vial of spirit gum. On the other side of the duo is her trademark everyday perfume—Florida Water. According to one of her diary entries, her first bottle was gifted to her by Lucille Ball at a birthday party. Though on special occasions, she wore Quelques Fleurs, a scent rich with royal history, legend, and lore.

Viviette was famously close to the late Marilyn Monroe for a period of time. After Marilyn's untimely passing, Viviette was once quoted as telling an overly inquisitive tabloid journalist, "Whatever did or didn't happen, whoever is or isn't responsible, none of it will bring her back. Let the woman rest in peace, and don't ever breathe her name in my presence again."

Viviette was a pistol.

A beautiful, glamorous sharpshooter of a woman who wore her attitude like an accessory.

On the opposite side of the vanity is Viviette's makeup collection featuring compacts of false lashes, Coty Airspun powder, Erno Laszlo foundations, and her signature lip color: Revlon Cherries in the Snow. Little glass bottles of Dura-Gloss nail polish sit pretty in classic shades like Rich Geranium, Bold Scarlet, and Shimmering Raspberry. Wells said his grandmother never left the house without painted nails and lipstick to match. That was her signature look—along with ornate and oversized cocktail rings. She called them her "conversation pieces." Whenever she found herself stuck in a mind-numbing exchange with someone, she'd seize the first opportunity to change the subject, prattling off some embellished tale about the history of whichever ring she happened to slip on that day.

I slide one of her diaries off the vanity counter and flip to a random page in the middle, feasting my eyes on her delicate handwriting with its tall swoops and slight slant to the right.

A woman's infallible armor is her beauty. One can and should use her exterior as a weapon whenever necessary. It can draw people in just as easily as it can send them cowering in corners. With the right colors and techniques, a lady can place the focus on her lips—when she wants to be heard. Or on her eyes—when she wants to seduce (or be seduced). With the right body language, one can command a room or disappear into a crowd unnoticed. A powerful woman should be a brilliant chameleon, a skilled people reader, a quick-thinking conversationalist, and a force to be reckoned with if she wants to succeed in this industry . . . in this life, too.

I can almost hear her speaking these words in her mid-Atlantic accent, with its soft vowels and dropped r's, her voice sharp and sweet at the same time. A nostalgic nod to simpler times.

I close the leather-bound journal, leave her vanity exactly the way I found it, and head to her dressing room. Flicking the light switch, I make my way to the center of the generous space, standing beneath a sparkling chandelier dripping with multi-faceted Baccarat crystals.

If these Dior and Balmain dresses could talk, I imagine they'd have stories for days.

I trace my fingertips softly along a row of tweed Chanel blazers—neatly organized by colors ranging from bold to neutral and everything in between. Inhaling the scent of long-faded perfume and time, I make my way to her shoe collection, marveling at how petite her feet were. In the farthest corner stands a dress form on wheels—one shaped with her exact bust, waist, and hip measurements before she retired from the spotlight altogether.

I was eight years old the day I first watched Viviette's Academy Award–winning performance in *Society Girl*. I was home with the flu and Gigi had control of the remote, wasting no time tuning it to the channel with the black-and-white movies. Within the first five minutes, I was transfixed. And by the time my next birthday rolled around, I'd seen all thirty-eight of Viviette's feature films. Twice. The fact that I'm standing in Westhaven—*in her personal dressing room*—fills me with gratitude and wonderment, a high I'm certain I'll never quite feel again in my career.

Regardless, inspiration eludes me today.

I turn off the glimmering chandelier, close the door, and exit Viviette's suite.

I need fresh air and a long walk to clear my head.

A few minutes later, I'm laced up and trekking down the front walk toward the iron gate emblazoned with Westhaven's signature *W* encircled with bronzed roses. Once I hit the sidewalk, I pass an unfamiliar car parked in the side lot—where the estate's employees park.

It must be Glenna's car as the badge dangling from the rearview mirror shows the cornflower-blue Visiting Nurses logo.

Up ahead, a man rides past on a bicycle that looks much too small for him. Or perhaps he's simply too big for the bike. With inky black hair, a linebacker's build, and eyes like two soulless voids, he cranes his neck and stares in my direction when he cruises past.

He doesn't smile or say hello. He doesn't nod or wave. He simply watches me.

It sends a shiver down my spine that doesn't dissipate until he returns his attention to the road ahead of him.

There aren't many bicyclists in this neighborhood. It's mostly luxury imports, sports cars, and extra-long SUVs carting children to and from their private schools and sports clubs.

Once he's out of sight, I brush it off, though an unsettling chill lingers just beneath my skin.

Continuing on my walk, my thoughts turn to Sylvie. I should check on her later, though it's not my place—not to mention I'd hate to make things worse. I feel awful for upsetting her, and I'd love a chance to explain and apologize, but the odds of seeing her again—one on one—are slim to none.

This morning was a fluke.

Pure happenstance.

A perfect storm of various factors that will likely never occur again.

Strolling down our leafy street, past flawlessly trimmed hedges that hide hacienda-style ranches and Spanish-inspired mansions filthy rich with history, I dig Sylvie's note from my pocket.

My grandfather used to tell me, *"Not every question has an answer."*

The sentiment always bothered my curious soul, and I've spent my entire life proving how wrong he was.

If a person looks hard enough, there are answers for everything.

4

JADE

"Excuse me," I call out to the raven-haired woman pushing the stroller half a block ahead of me. "Excuse me, I think you dropped this?"

She glances back from over her shoulder, and I wave the stuffed elephant I found on the sidewalk.

Her full lips arch into a grateful smile and her dark eyes soften. "Oh, my goodness. Yes, that's definitely ours."

Maneuvering her stroller, she heads my way in her skintight athleisure and neon-yellow sneakers.

"Thank you so much," she says when I hand it off. "We'd have been looking all over for this thing tonight, wouldn't we, Lily?"

She places the stuffed animal in the arms of a toddler who shares her same shiny jet-black hair and deep chocolate irises.

"I'm Portia," she says.

"Jade. Nice to meet you." In the brief time I've lived here, I've yet to meet a single neighbor. With all the gates and hedges, it's rare to see anyone outside of their own residential bubble.

"You live at Westhaven, don't you? I've seen you coming and going a few times . . ." She offers a sly smile.

I lift a brow. She's one of those women who don't miss a thing.

It takes one to know one.

"I do," I say, head cocked.

"We're next door to you . . . in the white colonial."

"Ah. With the red peonies," I say before quickly adding, "I can see them from my office window. They're gorgeous."

"You like them? I've never been a fan of red flowers. Red is such an angry color to me. But those things have been there for decades and my husband won't let me rip them out. The original owner planted them and my husband's all about preserving the charm and integrity of the home. His words. Though he wasn't so concerned with preserving all this charm and integrity when we renovated the main bath last year. The shower alone looks like it's out of some futuristic space movie. I don't know what half of the buttons and knobs do . . ."

She rambles on, rolling her eyes, and chuckling, and then she pauses, as if she's waiting for me to interject some minor complaint about my husband. I mean, I would if I could, but so far Wells has been nothing short of perfect.

Then again, we're still in our honeymoon phase. I don't expect these waters to always be this Botox-smooth.

"Your house is all original, right?" she asks after an uncomfortable bit of silence. "Wells mentioned something about turning the home into a museum someday."

"That's exactly what he wants to do," I say. "How long have you lived here?"

"In Brentwood? Or LA."

"Both."

"Twenty in LA . . . five . . . no, six years in this house." Her face scrunches as she looks to the side, and I mentally calculate that she's been here long enough to have known Wells and Sylvie before her accident. "You?"

"About two months in this house," I say, pointing to the bronzed gate behind me. It's unfitting to call the breathtaking monstrosity a *house* when it's so much more than that. It's a secluded world all its own. A priceless time capsule. A golden-age American castle.

Most days I still feel like a visitor.

Or a vacationer.

Maybe one day it'll feel like home.

"Have you met everyone yet?" She motions toward a few houses. "The Shafers . . . the Briggs . . . the Patels . . . the Anistons—no relation to Jennifer, in case you're wondering."

Snorting a chuckle, I shake my head. "Haven't met a soul."

She waves a flattened hand. "Don't worry, you're not missing much. This isn't the kind of street that has block parties and BBQs. You'll need to head to Tarzana or Encino for that. Though I will say, we spent quite a bit of time with Wells and Sylvie—before her accident, of course. They were lovely. Such a shame what happened . . ."

Portia tosses her glossy black hair over one shoulder before bending over the stroller to tie her daughter's unlaced sneakers. There isn't a single fine line or blemish on her flawless olive skin. Like most of the women around here, she's ageless.

"Where'd you live before this?" she asks as she secures the bow on the second shoe. "Before moving to Westhaven, I mean."

"I had an apartment in West Hollywood," I say. "Definitely no neighborhood BBQs there."

"Back in Nebraska, whenever someone new moved to our street, we'd stop by with a plate of brownies the second the moving truck left. It was equal parts *welcome to the neighborhood* and also a way to scope out the newcomers. Can't do that here unless it's gluten-free, paleo, organic, keto-friendly, or whatever the latest craze is. Did you see that new bakery on La Brea that uses cauliflower in everything?" Her expression sours. "I'll try just about anything, but the buck stops at cauliflower cupcakes."

I've known this woman all of three minutes and I already adore her. She's chatty and lacks a filter—people like her make for the most entertaining conversations. They spill all kinds of tea without even realizing it.

I'd kill to pick her brain sometime about Sylvie.

Wells doesn't speak about her often, and I haven't determined if he's doing it out of respect to me or as a way to compartmentalize the tragedy they experienced. Perhaps it's a little of both. Regardless, I never pry. I don't want to seem insecure nor do I want to pick the scab off an old wound of his.

"I'm with you. Cauliflower desserts are a hard pass," I say.

"Right?" She leans in, brushing her hand against my arm like she's known me much longer than five minutes. "People here act like a little Betty Crocker box mix every once in a while will kill them—or wreck their figure. Same difference to some I guess."

Portia's taut, toned shoulders and narrow waist suggest she's no stranger to spending regular time in the gym, but she seems like the type to treat herself. That or it's a classic case of good genes. Some people have all the luck.

"You're making me nostalgic for Kansas, and I haven't missed that place in years," I say.

"Ah, you're from the Midwest, too?" Her brows lift and her face lights. "Love it. How'd you end up all the way out here?"

"It's a long story," I say with a polite smile. I don't want to take too much of her time, nor do I want to jog down a long and winding memory lane involving an ex-boyfriend I'd give anything to forget.

Another time maybe.

Portia checks the shiny screen of her snow-white smartwatch, her lips bunching at one side. "I need to finish my walk and then get Lily to our Mommy-and-Me music class. You going to be around later? I'd love to chat more . . ."

"Yeah, I should be." Surreal morning aside, I'd almost forgotten Wells was out of town. This is the first time we've ever been apart, or at least sleeping in different states. As much as I adore the man, I'd be lying if I said I wasn't looking forward to having a little bit of breathing room. I'd planned to take a hot bath, order Thai takeout, and lose myself in a marathon binge of *Outlander*—just like old times—but I'm not about to turn Portia down.

She slides her iPhone from the side pocket of her leggings and thumbs in a six-digit code to unlock it.

"What's your number?" she asks without looking up.

I rattle off my digits.

"Perfect," she says. "I'll text you later."

With that, she offers a casual finger wave before careening her stroller around and continuing on her way. We're headed in the same direction, but I take a left at the next corner to avoid following behind her like some weird creeper.

Portia seems genuine—and impressively perceptive—and I can only imagine the light she might be able to shed on Sylvie's situation. Maybe she knows something . . . maybe not. But if there's anything I've learned in all of my years studying human beings at their finest and at their worst, it's that the hardest truths prefer to hide, but sometimes they're just a well-crafted question away.

I was twelve the first time I snuck into my older sister's room and happened upon her open diary, which she'd left carelessly sticking out from between her mattress and box spring in her haste to meet up with a friend at the city pool.

Two hours later, I was rich with knowledge of a side of Janessa no one knew existed. Crushes, enemies, girl drama mostly. Rants about our mother from time to time. Gripes about me peppered in for good measure. As time went on, it was between those very pages that I learned when my goody-two-shoes star-student sister smoked weed for the first time. When she lost her virginity at age fifteen to her best friend's boyfriend. When she pawned Mom's beloved antique pearl earrings out of spite after Mom refused to buy her the candy apple–red Mustang convertible she wanted and got her a fuel-efficient gray Honda instead.

From the outside looking in, Janessa was a model daughter. Beautiful, intelligent, ambitious overachiever. But I knew the real her; the one hiding behind her picture-perfect veneer and living scandalously on the pages of a cheap little dollar-store diary.

My fixation on unburying secrets only intensified from then on, and I quickly became obsessed with digging up piles upon piles of dirt on every unsuspecting soul who waltzed into my life—and I became terrifyingly good at it. So much so, that all of my friends (and classmates) would seek me out to dig up intel on anyone and everyone . . . cheating boyfriends or girlfriends, parents, teachers mostly.

The advent of smartphones and social media made my sleuthing a walk in the park.

I never dreamed that my insatiability for knowledge and fascination with people would lead to a career as a biographer, but preparation met opportunity and here I am.

I finish my walk, head home, return to my desk, and make my dreaded call to my agent, ready to break the news that I'm going to miss my due date next month. Only her first question for me has nothing to do with my deadline.

"Has Wells read what you have so far?" Julie asks.

"Not yet," I say. "He's been buried with work."

"Maybe you should have him give it a quick look. Just to be safe . . ."

Part of the publishing contract stipulated that Wells reserved the right to pull the plug on the project at any time during the writing process. Until it's sent off for editing, nothing's set in stone. And should he put the kibosh on this, I'd have to pay back my six-figure advance in full. Of course, my publisher could still move forward with the book if they wanted to . . . it would just be considered an "unauthorized biography," which would hinder sales and tarnish the author brand I've worked so hard at establishing.

Not to mention the consequences it would have on my marriage.

I could never do that to him.

But I'm not worried. Wells specifically chose me for this project because he loved the book I wrote about nineteenth-century railroad heiress Georgina Peregrine and the scandalous and tragic Peregrine family dynasty. It's the entire reason we met. He happened upon a copy of *The Misfortunate Peregrines* at an airport bookstore, and by the time his flight landed several hours later, he was calling my agent to arrange a meeting.

He wants this book to happen just as much as I do.

"He's traveling for work this week," I say, "but when he gets back, I'll have him read a few chapters."

Julie exhales into the receiver. "Please do. And send me what you have so far when you get a chance."

"Of course." Heat creeps up my neck. She already knows I'm behind, but she doesn't exactly know just how behind I am. "I'll send you my manuscript by the end of today. It's going to be a little shorter than what you're probably expecting . . ."

"I'll watch for your email," she says before hanging up.

I anchor myself in front of my laptop, all but shackling my ankles to my chair as I stare at a white Word document with a blinking cursor and a chapter header. I finish two full chapters over the next two hours before breaking to stretch my legs and grab a Honeycrisp apple to snack on.

I'm approaching the middle of the book—which coincides with Viviette's middle age. She was forty-three when she gave birth to her first and only child, Mary Claire. From what I've gathered in her journal entries, Viviette was always told she couldn't have children so falling pregnant at that age was both a blessing and a shock—especially since the father was rumored to be a married costar; one who remains unnamed to this day, though there's no shortage of theories and speculations.

Of course, Viviette's studio and PR agency worked arduously to hide the disreputable pregnancy from the public eye, keeping Viviette behind closed doors once she started to show. The instant Mary Claire was born, they drafted up a press release announcing Viviette had "adopted" a little girl from an orphanage in Mississippi.

I page through my research notes until I get to Mary Claire's phone number.

I've been putting this off for a while now. If she were any other person, I'd have called her long ago and asked her all my questions, but the idea of ringing up a mother-in-law I've yet to meet just to grill her about the complicated relationship she had with her own mother feels . . . heavy and invasive. Personal, too, given the fact that the Westmore family is now technically my family.

I type her number into my phone, hit the green button, and place it on speaker. My heartbeat whooshes in my ears with every ring and my mouth runs dry when I attempt to swallow. There's a chance she could hang up on me after I introduce myself—it wouldn't be the first time. But there's an equal chance she'd be thrilled to share her stories. Most of the time, people love to contribute their memories—unless they're too painful. It happens from time to time.

"Hello, you've reached Mary Claire Westmore. Please leave a message after the tone," her automated greeting plays after four rings. Her voice is pleasant, shockingly maternal, like a sitcom mom.

I clear my throat before the beep. "Hi, Mary Claire. This is Jade . . . Wells's wife. Wells said he mentioned to you previously that I'm working on a biography about your mother, and I was hoping you might have some time to meet and go over some details about her life? Thanks so much, and I hope to hear from you soon."

I hang up, return to my Word doc, and reread and edit my last two chapters. Until I hear from Mary Claire, this stage of the biography is in limbo. I could add a few things and fill in the blanks later, but having a fully painted picture would make it easier to structure this segment.

It's a quarter past eight when my phone rings.

"Hey." I answer the second I see it's my husband.

"Sorry I'm calling so late," Wells says with an exhaled groan. I picture him kicking off his leather loafers and sinking into a chair in his hotel room. "It's been a long day."

"I bet. Everything going okay so far?"

"It is. Only thing that would make it better is if you were here with me."

I'd thought about accompanying him, but I didn't want to be a distraction, nor did I want to hole up in a hotel room for seven days, waiting all day for him to come rescue me at the end of the night. After a couple of days in a hotel, I tend to go stir-crazy. Plus, I need to be around Viviette's things while I write. Sitting in some Marriott suite would be slightly less than inspiring.

"The week will go by fast," I tell him. "You'll be home before you know it."

"How's the book coming?"

"It's coming . . . I actually left a message for your mother this afternoon about interviewing her."

"She didn't answer when you called?"

I pick at a loose thread in my leggings. "Nope."

Wells had mentioned once before that Mary Claire was—for lack of a better word—flaky. A former wild child, she had Wells when she was barely nineteen. Practically a baby herself. Apparently Viviette wasted no time adopting Wells and Mary Claire wasted no time fleeing the nest with her newfound freedom. Their relationship has been on shaky ground ever since, which I imagine plays a part in the fact that Wells has yet to introduce us.

"Let me know if you need me to call her," he says. "She might answer for me."

"Will do," I say. "I met a neighbor today . . . Portia . . . I didn't get her last name."

He's quiet.

"She lives in the white house next door with the red peonies," I add in case he needs his memory jogged. He, much like everyone else in this neighborhood, tends to spend his free time in his own residential bubble.

"Oh, right. Portia," he says as if he's suddenly remembering her—which is interesting given the fact that she implied they used to get together when he was married to Sylvie. There's a chance she was exaggerating. That's another thing people do en masse out here. Connections and name-dropping are forms of currency in these parts. It isn't unusual for someone to speak about an acquaintance as if they're a good friend.

I let it go. It's been a long day for both of us.

"Hate to cut this short, but I'm going to make myself a nightcap and turn in for the night," he says. "Early morning tomorrow."

"Yes, please get some rest. You sound exhausted."

"Love you," he says.

"Love you, too." I hang up, ignoring the gaping hole in my middle that accompanies me in the absence of his voice.

I've always prided myself on being hyper-independent. Married life was never a goal of mine, and dating was only something I did to pass the time on an occasional lonely Saturday night.

And then came Wells—ruining my plans to live my days as a reclusive spinster in some house by the sea.

Trekking to the bathroom in our shared suite, I uncap a bottle of his cologne and spritz it in the air. Pulling the intoxicating woody scent into my lungs, I close my eyes and picture his handsome face. Those hooded whiskey-hazel eyes with the fringe of dark lashes. The cleft in his chin. His thick, sandy hair always combed neatly, more fitted for a WWII GI coming home from the war.

My stomach somersaults at the thought of seeing him again in six days, of settling back into our comfortable little routine where he brings me tea in the morning and I greet him with a kiss fit for a silver screen at the end of the day.

My phone chimes, yanking me from my wistful reverie, and I tap the message icon to find a text from a local number along with a photo of a bottle of pinot noir and two stemless wineglasses.

> Hey! It's Portia with the red peonies! We met earlier today. ;) I can't drink this whole thing by myself. Correction—I shouldn't drink this whole thing by myself. You busy?

Speak of the devil.

I write back, letting her know I'm on my way. And then I trek to the breakfast nook, gathering the last of the Casa Blanca lilies and placing them in a vase with water—a makeshift gift for my hostess. Besides, I'm about to politely yet shamelessly grill her about my husband's first wife—it's only fair she gets something out of the deal. Of course, if I'm wrong about her being an unfiltered catalog of information, I'll drop it. I won't press her too hard. Those kinds of situations always backfire, and I'd hate to make a terrible impression on Portia when we hit it off so well earlier. Besides, I could use a friend with Midwestern roots. We're not terribly hard to come by out here, but genuine connections are.

I make my way to Portia's, flowers in hand and fingers crossed so hard they hurt.

5

JADE

"Screw it." Portia throws her hands in the air before rising from her overstuffed sofa. Turning, she motions for me to follow her. "I'm opening another bottle."

We've been conversing for an hour now, and we've yet to broach the topic of Sylvie. I've been waiting for a natural segue or the perfect place to switch gears, but we're having such a nice time there's no need to rush.

Empty wineglass in hand, I follow her into the kitchen, where she makes her way between two marble islands and retrieves a chilled magnum of Riesling from a glass-front fridge. I try to picture this space in the daytime, natural light flooding in through the wall of windows above her sink. But it's dark outside and other than a flickering scented candle and the light above her baby-blue La Cornue range, it's dark in here, too.

"I've been saving this one for a special occasion," she says as she inserts the corkscrew and gives it a twist. Her messy hair is piled into a loose bun at the crown of her head, save for a few dark strands that frame her heart-shaped face.

"Isn't that the equivalent of four bottles of wine?" I clap my hand over my mouth and stand back as she pulls the cork.

There's no way the two of us can put a dent in this tonight.

"You don't have any plans in the morning, do you?" She twists the cork off the screw and tosses it aside. Without another word, she reaches for my empty glass and fills it almost to the top. "Drink a Gatorade and take two Advil before bed. Your hangover won't stand a chance. Works every time. Try it and thank me tomorrow. You said you write books about old movie stars, right? Like that's your full-time job?"

I nod, watching as she fills her glass so full it nearly spills over the sides. "Among other notable people . . . heiresses, nobles, visionaries . . ."

"I bet you have all kinds of fascinating stories floating around in that head of yours." She takes a careful sip before sliding my glass closer to me. "Ones you haven't written about yet."

"Might have a few . . ."

Her dark eyes sparkle as she loops her hand into my elbow and leads me back to her white-on-white living room.

"Old Hollywood gossip is my guilty pleasure," she says. "And since my husband's at the condo tonight, I can geek out as much as I want in my own house."

"You can't geek out around him?"

She peers up at the ceiling for a half second before blowing a short breath between her lips.

"God no," she says. "He gets secondhand embarrassment whenever I bring up any of that stuff to other people. On one of our first dates, I made him go on one of those movie stars' homes bus tours, you know? Anyway, I thought he was going to die of humiliation."

She's chuckling. I'm not.

"I don't understand how that embarrasses him . . . you live in Los Angeles and he works in the entertainment industry." I mentally run through all the details she shared with me over the past hour: his name is Lee Solano. He's an entertainment lawyer who dabbles in producing—whatever that means. He's fifty and never wanted kids but now he thinks Lily hung the moon—at least when he's home. Lately he's been staying at their condo in downtown LA because it's closer to his office. Or that's the excuse he's given her.

Portia's sense of humor about these things could easily be a defense mechanism—or survival technique.

If she weren't laughing, perhaps she'd be crying.

"He thinks it's cringey." She shrugs before lowering herself onto the plush sofa.

I take the spot across from her. "How is a passion for local history cringey?"

Portia winces, her head tilting from one side to the other as if she's searching for the right words.

"Let me put it this way," she finally says. "Lee says if I were a man, I'd be a forty-year-old bachelor living in his mom's basement with Frank Sinatra posters on the wall. I'd be the kind of guy who unironically wears a fedora. The kind who goes to classic car shows and takes pictures with the Marilyn Monroe impersonators."

Lee sounds like a douche.

A judgmental, unoriginal one at that.

The kind of guy who makes his wife feel small so that he can feel big.

I bury my true feelings behind a sip of wine and a smile. It's not my style to sit on her sofa, drink her wine, and speak ill of her husband.

Portia rolls her eyes. "Lee's kind of a wet blanket sometimes. I figure it's only a matter of time before he leaves me for that blonde he's been screwing behind my back. It's always the damn blondes—no offense."

She speaks as casually as if she were remarking about the weather.

I almost choke on my Riesling. "Wait. What?"

This time she doesn't chuckle. "I pretend I don't know about *her* just like he pretends he doesn't know Lily's not his biological daughter."

The room is a vacuum of silence as I struggle to find the words—any words at all—to say.

A handful of shiny new questions dance on my tongue, but I forbid myself from asking a single one as we're still getting to know each other, still making first impressions. This stage is delicate, and I like her.

"Sorry, sorry." Portia waves her hand, her delicate gold bracelets jingling. "I have a bad habit of oversharing. You probably didn't need to know all of that. Or any of it, really." Her attention falls to her lap for a second. "I guess I just—"

"You don't need to apologize," I say. If I were sitting next to her, I'd lean in and place a reassuring hand on her knee. *"At all."*

"Sooner or later you'll meet Lee, and you'll see how he and Lily look nothing alike, and people get curious . . ." Her voice trails off. ". . . I just like to get it out there, you know. It's better to talk about it, than to be talked about. That's my motto anyway."

"Portia," I say. "You don't have to explain—"

"I know. But I want to. I'm an open book. Always have been."

Our eyes catch and hers turn glassy before she blinks the dampness away. A woman who can go from smiling and laughing to rolling her eyes to shedding tears all within the span of a few moments is likely not in a good place.

"I don't have a lot of friends these days," she adds with a sigh. "The older you get, the harder it is to meet people, you know? And then to put in the time and effort to maintain those friendships. Add being a stay-at-home mom to the mix, and it's just impossible sometimes."

She isn't wrong. Making friends in your twenties is an ever-evolving shit show that's only amplified in your thirties as everyone gets married and starts families and moves to random cities for random jobs and you never hear from them again. Perhaps there's hope for us in our forties and beyond.

"I can't relate to the stay-at-home-mom part, but I know how lonely it can get," I say. "We both work from home in a way. It's isolating."

My high school friends and I scattered like leaves to the wind, going off to various colleges and trade schools after graduation. Then there were my friends at Northern Norvell University, who kept in touch only long enough to send wedding invites post-graduation. Once their "real" lives kicked off, it was crickets.

Since moving here, I've had a revolving door of friends and acquaintances. I'll get the random dinner invite text here or there, but no one here seems to be interested in any kind of authentic or lasting relationship. Only disposable, surface-level friendships. It's part of why I find dead people far more interesting than the ones alive today. The dead ones have already lived a full life with a beginning, middle, end, and twists along the way. Their stories are already completed and ready to be explored and dissected—save for Viviette's story, which has always been mysterious and peppered with blanks. She was notoriously private and her camp shot down anyone who tried to write any semblance of a book about her.

"Lee says I always come on too strong and that's why no one ever sticks around." Portia grabs a tissue from a leather-covered tissue box on the coffee table. Dabbing the corner of her eyes, she gives me an apologetic smile with a glint of shame in her eyes. "God, I don't know why I'm getting so emotional. It's got to be the wine. It's the wine, right? I *never* cry. Wait. I ran out of my Lexapro a few nights ago. It's got to be that. Ugh. Okay."

In an instant, the confident ray of sunshine Portia has proven to be all day vanishes, and I'm left with a woman just as fragile and life-worn as anyone else.

We all wear masks.

And sooner or later those masks come off.

"This wine is incredible by the way," I change the subject and take a generous gulp. "What was the special occasion you were saving this for?"

"I'm sorry, I think I just heard the baby monitor . . . I'll be right back." Portia disappears from the sofa into the dark hall before I hear her padding up the stairs. She returns a few minutes later. "Apparently Lily woke up because she dropped her elephant from the crib. I swear it's like she has ESP or something. She always knows when I wake up earlier than her or when I've snuck pureed sweet potatoes into her applesauce or when I try and swap out her favorite pacifier for a newer one. Can't get anything past her."

I'm not sure what else to say besides the classic, "She's going to give you a run for your money when she's older."

I know nothing about babies or toddlers, but I'm no stranger to tension-riddled mother-daughter relationships. Perhaps I could be of some use in the advice department in another fifteen or twenty years.

I think of Mary Claire and the strain she put Viviette through. By Mary Claire's teenage years, Viviette would have been in her late fifties. I doubt she had the energy to stay up all night waiting for her rebellious daughter to come home, nor did she have the patience to tolerate her disrespectful attitude.

"So you said you used to spend time with Wells and Sylvie?" I shotgun my question because it's starting to get late. Besides, we could use a good topic change.

Portia studies me before tucking her legs beneath her. "We did. Several times actually. We were actually discussing doing a couples' weekend in Sonoma before Sylvie had her accident. Nothing set in stone, just throwing the idea around. Ugh. Anyway, the whole thing was so tragic. You think you have your whole life ahead of you and then it changes in the blink of an eye."

"I don't really know much about her. Wells doesn't talk much about that period of his life."

Her eyes grow round and her back straightens. "Really? Like he pretends she doesn't exist or what? She lives in the guesthouse, right?"

"She does. And when he's home, he checks on her daily," I say, "but I meant he doesn't talk about her to *me*."

"That doesn't bother you?" She wears the pinched expression of a nosy housewife, but I don't take it to heart. It's a valid question. "When Lee and I first got married, we talked about our exes all the time. We wanted to analyze where things went wrong so we wouldn't be doomed to repeat our old mistakes." Portia lets out a single, heady laugh before taking a drink. "A strategy that clearly blew up in our faces."

"Why do you stay if he's cheating on you and makes fun of your interests?" The alcohol coursing through my warm veins has hindered my self-restraint. My question is pointed and personal, but Portia's an open book and open-book types love nothing more than to spill their contents.

It's half the fun for them.

"Look at this place," she says, voice soft as cashmere and dark irises gleaming. "I could never afford something like this on my own. If turning a blind eye while my husband gets his cock sucked by some flash-in-the-pan YouTube star means I get to raise my kids without having to worry about a single dime, then honey, I'll be as blind as a bat until the day my daughter graduates from college." Portia takes another drink, swallowing the remains of her wine. "Once upon a time, I thought I was head over heels in love with that man and I let his lawyers talk me into signing a god-awful prenup. I'd walk away with next to nothing, Jade. And I know damn well he'd contest Lily's paternity, which means she'd walk away with nothing, too."

"Fair enough. But why does *he* stay?" I ask. "I understand your side of things, but what's in it for him?"

"Million-dollar question. Control maybe? Pride? I'm wife number four—though maybe that says more about me than him." She rises, pointing to my glass. "You want a top off?"

"I'm good . . ."

She comes back a moment later, the magnum gripped tight in her manicured hand, and tops me off anyway.

"I have my theories, but at the end of the day, do they matter? And more importantly, do I care? I don't know that I do anymore." She settles onto her cushion again and reaches for her freshly poured wine. "Let's just say, I'm not losing sleep over any of it. Whatever's in the cards for me, I trust my future self can handle it."

"Love that," I say. "If I were writing your biography, I'd definitely quote that."

"What, the future self thing?" She laughs. "*Please.* I wish those were my words. I saw that on an inspirational calendar at a mall kiosk years ago."

"Either way, I'm impressed with your tenacity. I don't think many women could do what you're doing and still walk around with a smile on their face."

"Look, I was twenty when I had Oliver," she says, referring to the son she mentioned earlier in our conversation, when we were still working on our first glasses of wine and she had just put Lily down for the night. "Got knocked up my second year of Bible college by some guy I met at an off-campus party and never saw again. My ultraconservative parents—the same ones who'd greet new neighbors with Betty Crocker brownies—disowned me for not being married. We were on our own, just Olly and me. I had a cousin out here who said he could get me a job waiting tables at this hole-in-the-wall oyster bar in Venice, so I packed up Olly and everything I owned into my little blue Hyundai and we never looked back." Portia gathers a long, slow breath. "Of course I was young and stupid and terrible with money, so it took us a lot of years to get on our feet. A lot of working double shifts and weekends and praying the babysitter didn't cancel on me again. Eventually I worked my way into the finer restaurants—that's how I met Lee. He would come to Maude's in Beverly Hills every Friday for lunch, and he'd request me as his server. After several weeks of insanely big tips, I finally asked him when he was taking me out."

"Wow. So you made the first move?"

"Guilty," she says. "How's that for the world's most cliché love story? Anyway . . . how'd you meet Wells?"

"He'd been wanting to authorize a biography on his grandmother for years, but wasn't impressed with any of the writing samples he'd been given, and the whole idea sort of fell to the wayside once Sylvie had her accident. I guess last year he picked up one of my books at an airport and by the time he landed, he was contacting my agent to set up a meeting. We met for dinner a week later—just the two of us—and I guess you could say we hit it off."

"You just *hit it off*?" she asks. "Come on. You're going to have to give me more details than that. You're basically Cinderella in this equation. Where's the rest of the story?"

A dopey smile claims my face before I can stop it, but I don't care. Thinking about Wells sends me reeling every time. I hope this high never fades. For now, I'm clinging on to it with every fiber of my soul.

"He was impressed with my knowledge of his grandmother," I say, "and that segued into my love of old Hollywood history, which then intersected with his knowledge of Hollywood architectural history as well as a few stories from his childhood, and by the time the check was paid, we were hightailing it to his car. We spent all night driving around different neighborhoods sharing legends and lore and ogling all the charming old houses. After that, we drove to this overlook and talked until the sun came up."

Portia places her stemless glass on a coaster before leaning back and throwing her hands up.

"See. I wish Lee could hear this right now because he admires the hell out of Wells, and I'd die to see the look on his face when he learns Wells Westmore geeks out on *cringey* local history."

"Have you ever been inside Westhaven?" I ask.

"No," she says. "Sylvie always wanted to come here whenever we got together. I figured sooner or later the invite would go the other way, but . . . yeah, no."

"Really?" I squint. Everything I know about Sylvie suggests she had a robust social calendar. Given their high society wedding guest list and her love of all things entertaining, surely she'd have thrown a handful of parties there . . . or at the very least, hosted a friend or two.

"They were adamant about always coming here when we'd all get together," Portia says. "They were always restoring floors or refinishing something or other. I got the sense they were living in a construction zone."

I know Wells remodeled the kitchen, but that was years ago, before he'd married Sylvie. He mentioned it once when I asked why it was so dark. The space was filled with straight lines, espresso-tone woods, masculine hardware, black marble, and cold stainless steel appliances. It was a work of modern art, cohesive and appeasing enough to the eye, but it was a harsh contrast to the rest of the sun-drenched Spanish colonial estate and seemed better suited for a penthouse in Manhattan. I'd teasingly told him once that it needed a woman's touch, and he agreed. He even went so far as to say his grandmother would hate everything about the statement-making kitchen, but he had no choice but to update it if he wanted to get any practical use out of it and bring it up to code.

"I feel sort of . . . weird . . . asking this, but what were they like?" I ask, cutting to the chase as the clock ticks later. "Sylvie and Wells."

Portia sits forward, resting her elbows on the tops of her bony knees and staring past my shoulder, lost in thought for a moment.

"Well," she finally says. "Do you want the truth?"

"Nothing but."

"I don't know if I've ever met anyone as in sync as those two." Her rosy lips begin to move before she speaks again. "It was like they anticipated each other's every move, and on top of that, they were glued at the hip. You know that cheesy expression about finishing each other's sentences? That was them. And the way he looked at her . . ."

Portia sighs, clasping her hands over her heart.

Practically swooning.

"I'm sorry. I know we're talking about your husband," she says, "but you have to understand . . . being around the two of them was an *experience*. That's the simplest way I can put it. It was like watching some classic love story play out in real time, before our very eyes. It's like they were made for each other. Soulmates, if you believe in that stuff."

My heart breaks. But not for me . . . for my husband.

No wonder he keeps her near.

And no wonder he keeps her name out of his mouth in my presence.

She was the love of his life—a fact that isn't lost on me.

I can't imagine being in that position nor can I imagine handling it with an ounce of his tact and grace.

He can have respect for his ex and respect for me at the same time. There's no mutual exclusivity.

"I saw their wedding photos," I say. "Some of them anyway."

"So he won't talk about her to you, but he'll let you page through his wedding album?"

"Google," I say with a wink and a sly half smile. "Mostly."

Portia snorts. "Of course."

"I actually have a knack for digging up dirt on people," I say, "if you ever need me to do a little light sleuthing . . ."

"Should I be impressed or terrified?" she asks.

"I'm harmless." I swallow a mouthful of white wine. "Relatively."

Though Viviette herself might beg to differ. She wrote in a January 1957 diary entry that: "*An informed woman is the biggest threat to modern society—as she should be. It's why they want us dumbed down and docile. If we're in the kitchen with a baby on our hip or lying naked on our backs at night, we're too preoccupied to notice what's going on outside the home.*"

"What was Sylvie like?" I ask while we're still on the subject. "As a friend, I mean. As you knew her."

A lightness colors Portia's expressive eyes, yet at the same time, she releases a bittersweet sigh.

"She was kind," she says. "Funny. Personable. A chatterbox. You could talk to her for five minutes and somehow feel like you'd known her your whole life. She was also down to earth, humble. Not your typical Angeleno, even though she grew up in Culver City."

"Kind of sounds like you."

Her lips turn up at one side and she exhales a wistful sigh. "I really thought we were going to be good friends. It was like we were kindred souls in a way. Of course maybe that's just me *coming on too strong* as Lee likes to say, but I felt a connection with her. A true connection. Something I've never felt with anyone else, not even my husband. It was like we spoke the same language or we were cut from the same cloth."

"Did you visit her after the accident?"

Portia's lips flatten for a moment, and then she shakes her head.

"Wells wouldn't let anyone see her," she says before taking a sip.

"What?" I cock my head to the side. That doesn't sound like my husband at all. "Why not?"

"All I know is we reached out after we heard about everything, and he said they weren't taking visitors at that time. He said he'd let me know when I could see her again, but gosh . . . it's been years now. And I never wanted to pry. The more time that passed, the more it felt inappropriate to bother him, so I let it go. I figured he had enough on his plate. Now that ship has definitely sailed."

"Ugh. I'm so sorry," I say. "It must've been hard for you, not getting that closure."

"I'm sure he was just doing what he thought was best for her at the time," she says. "He was always protective of her, even before the accident. A little too protective in my opinion."

"Wells was overprotective?" We can't possibly be talking about the same man.

"God, yes. Security cameras everywhere, curfews. He always had to know where she was going and when she'd be back. I know he knew the passcode on her phone because I saw him checking it once when she'd received a text and was in the next room."

"She told you he gave her a curfew?" I ask.

"In not so many words, yes. She mentioned it once when she stopped over with some of my mail. She seemed upset that day, not her usual chipper self, and when I asked if she wanted to come in for a bit and talk, she said she couldn't stay long because Wells would wonder where she was and he liked her home before dark. That was the first and only time she ever mentioned anything like that, and unfortunately, that was one of the last times we spoke."

I wrinkle my nose and try to imagine my calm, quiet, gentle, and bookish husband as anything but. I've seen him catch house spiders and set them free more times than I can count. And he's never once asked for my phone passcode or made me feel like I was being monitored in any way. And sure there are cameras around the estate, but that's normal for places like Westhaven. The house is no stranger to random fans attempting to climb the gates to snap photos or to take self-guided tours around the premises.

"Are you sure she was . . ." I pause to collect my thoughts and choose my words carefully. "Of sound mind? I just . . . Wells has security cameras set up around the house for general safety reasons, and he's never once hounded me about my comings and goings or asked for any passwords to anything. The Wells you're describing—doesn't make sense. He's nothing like that."

"I know what I saw. I know what she said. That said, people change all the time," she says before leaning closer to the coffee table and throwing her hands up. "Though I will say, there was some grapevine talk about Sylvie having some sort of mental breakdown, becoming reclusive and paranoid. But talk is cheap so I always took it with a grain of salt. All I know is what *I* witnessed. Can't speak to the rest of it."

Before I have a chance to volley another question her way, our conversation is interrupted by the slamming of a door in the back of the house.

"Ah. That's Olly," Portia singsongs, wearing a smile that fades the instant she checks her watch. "And he's late. Again."

I can't begin to imagine what it's like raising a twenty-year-old and a one-year-old at the same time. She puts one to bed only to wait for the other one to come home.

"Feel free to help yourself to a refill while I have a little *chat* with my son."

"Oh, no, it's fine. I should get going anyway." I collect my glass and carry it to the sink, stopping in my tracks when I see a tall, dark shadow standing in front of the open fridge.

It only takes a moment for me to realize it's the same man who biked past me on my walk—the same man who stared me down until my entire body turned to ice.

Standing this close to him, I determine he must be at least six foot five, and I don't want to begin to guess his weight, but judging by the thick muscles bulging from his shirt, I'd wager that it's an impressive number. And he sure as hell doesn't look like the sweet and innocent freckle-faced *Olly* I'd pictured when she initially told me about her son.

Olly turns to face me, his eyes once again like two dark voids and his expression unreadable.

"Who're you?" His invasive stare drags the length of me, and there's a hint of resentment in his voice, as if he's annoyed by my presence.

"Oliver," Portia speaks his name between clenched teeth before rushing to stand between us. "Don't be rude. This is Jade, our next-door neighbor. Jade, this is my son, Olly."

"Wonderful to meet you, Olly." I extend my hand.

He looks away, then turns back to the fridge. Grabbing a carton of orange juice, he unscrews the lid and takes a series of generous gulps.

"I'm so sorry," Portia mouths to me before placing her hand on his rounded shoulder. Her cheeks are flushed, though it's impossible to know if it's the wine or sheer embarrassment.

"It's fine," I mouth back.

"Olly, let's go have a quick talk in the next room about manners," she says. I can't help but wonder if she always speaks to him like he's a child or if she's doing it for my sake. Turning back to me, she adds, "I'll text you tomorrow, Jade."

"Perfect." I show myself out and head home. The sky that was painted shades of pink and creamy orange mere hours ago is now pitch black without a single star in sight. Meanwhile, the soft scents of night-blooming jasmine, lemon trees, and Portia's red peonies dance on the tepid summer breeze; a serene ending to a rollercoaster of a day.

I pass our private parking lot on the way. Glenna's car is now gone and a gray SUV with a Visiting Nurses parking pass has taken its place.

The house is quiet, somehow managing to feel emptier than before. Or maybe it's Wells's notable absence. Either way, something is missing.

A few minutes later, I'm upstairs, washing the day off my face and changing into the periwinkle cashmere nightgown Wells got me for Christmas last year. Our satin sheets get cold at night, and without him beside me I'll need the added warmth.

I think about calling Wells just to hear his voice, but it's too late now. With the time difference, he's likely fast asleep. And if he isn't, he should be.

Before I turn in for the night, I peek out of the blinds, toward the caretaker's cottage, thinking about everything Portia said tonight about Wells and Sylvie being soulmates joined at the hip, finishing each other's sentences.

Her little house is dark, save for the bedroom light, and her curtains are drawn wide. From here I can tell her bed is still made from this morning and the chair next to it is still free from dirty clothes. I'm about to pull my curtains closed when Sylvie's slender figure suddenly appears in front of her window.

Startled, I gasp, hiding behind a velvet drape. It takes a moment to catch my breath, but when I do, I steal another glimpse. The light pouring from behind her makes her nothing but a shadowy figure with no discernible features, but I know it's her.

She stands still as a statue, making it impossible to know what she's looking at.

I think of Portia's comments earlier, about Wells's purported possessiveness and Sylvie's rumored mental breakdown.

And then I think of the slip of paper.

And that word.

Run.

That alone tells me she understands more than she gets credit for.

That she's not a catatonic bag of bones.

If there's any skill I've honed over the course of my writing career, it's the art of giving a voice to those without one. While my subjects tend to be deceased and Sylvie is very much alive, it doesn't change the fact that there are silent thoughts behind those knowing eyes.

Thoughts that need a voice.

I pull my curtains closed, climb under the sheets, and roll to my side, running my hand along the cool, bare space where Wells usually sleeps.

Tonight there's an undeniable chill in the air.

I pull the covers tight around me and attempt to quiet the questions dizzying my mind. If my husband were here, he'd be propped up on a stack of pillows. His dim book light would be illuminating the pages of the hardback novel in his hands, and the last thing I'd see before falling asleep would be the shadowy outline of his striking profile and the way his lips move ever so slightly as he reads.

I'd sidle up to him, bury my head against his shoulder, and pass out listening to his steady breaths and the occasional soft flick of paper.

Portia mentioned earlier that she and her husband openly talked about their exes in the beginning of their relationship. My entire life, I've prided myself on my openness and my ability to find the perfect time to ask a hard-hitting question, and the men in my romantic life were never the exception.

Yet when it comes to Wells, I find myself more tight-lipped than ever. When we were first beginning to spend time together, I'd ask him anything and everything I could possibly think of about his grandmother—personal or no. I was researching so all bets were off. But when we started having feelings for one another, I couldn't bring myself to dig too deep below his pristine surface. Not quickly and all at once. I didn't want to scare him off—to risk losing the intense connection that was happening so fast it made my head spin.

Naturally, I wanted to know everything about him. I was obsessed. Consumed. Still am to a degree. But I've managed to rein it in.

Early on, I promised myself I'd sit down and enjoy the proverbial ride with this one, that I wouldn't go searching for "spoilers" or looking for reasons to speed up our inevitable demise.

Some of my greatest idols did the very same thing.

And that's pretty much the whole thing about relationships—you can't read the last page first. You can't skip to the end. You have to go in blind and hope for the best.

I pull Wells's pillow against my chest, take a deep breath, and do just that.

6

JADE

I wipe the sleep from my eyes as I cautiously lug my laptop, phone, notebook, and mug of Earl Grey into Viviette's suite Wednesday morning. My bones ache, unrested, my head hammers, and my thoughts are foggy. Yesterday's events did a number on me. I normally wouldn't eat or drink in this room, but I'm in desperate need of both caffeine and inspiration at the same time.

I set up camp at Viviette's writing desk—an alleged gift from her *Virginia and Me* costar Marlon Brando, and I open my manuscript, scrolling to an early chapter about her ambitious twenties, when she was new and unknown, as fearless as she was determined.

After reaching for one of her leather journals, I gently page through her entries until I find a section that corresponds with this period of her life.

The other day, I auditioned for a part as a background dancer for an RKO feature film. The call sheet requested blondes only, five foot five to five foot eight, twenty-four or younger, with dancing experience required. One girl—Martha—showed up with peroxide burns on her scalp and hair that was more orange than blonde. She was also on the shorter side, walking with her nose held high as if she thought it'd help her gain a couple of inches.

That's the difference between women like her and women like me—I go where I'm needed. I don't waste time going where I'm not wanted.

I had half a mind to pull the poor thing aside and give her a few words of advice, but she left the casting room in a fit of tears with her face buried in her hands. I can only imagine what they said to her in there. Casting directors don't have time for niceties, not when there's a line of hopefuls out the door and down the block.

But I've been thinking about Martha ever since. Especially her desperation. Deep down I suppose we're all desperate for something be it love, attention, or validation.

Some of us simply do a better job at hiding it, is all.

I'm tweaking a handful of paragraphs when my phone rings. Wells texted me this morning, letting me know he'd call me when they break for lunch, but it's barely nine thirty—and the name flashing across my screen isn't Wells . . . it's Mary Claire.

If I wasn't awake a second ago, I am now.

Sitting up, I clear my throat, brush my hair behind one ear, and take the call.

"Hello?" I answer.

"Yes, hi. You must be Jade?" The same pleasant voice from her greeting yesterday fills my ear. "This is Mary Claire. You left me a message yesterday? Sorry I missed your call. I was with my hiking club in Runyon Canyon. Anyway, you said you had some questions for your book?"

"Right, thank you so much for getting back to me," I say. "Was hoping we could get together sometime soon so I could ask you a few things about your mother and get a better understanding about your childhood?"

She's quiet for a beat, and cold sweat blankets my forehead when it occurs to me that perhaps she isn't on board with the authorized biography. Then again, I'm sure Wells would've mentioned that by now.

"Of course," she says with a smile in her soft voice. "I'm free later this afternoon if that would work for you? Maybe around four? There's a little coffee shop down the road from me. I can send you the location. You don't mind coming here, do you? I just hate the traffic on Wilshire that time of day."

"Yes, that's perfect." I tamp down the excitement in my tone and remind myself to be professional. Never mind that this is the first time I've ever spoken to my mother-in-law or the fact that she's the closest living link we have to Viviette other than Wells. Electric excitement rings through me, settling in my fingertips as I grab a pen and jot down "four o'clock—Mary Claire" lest I forget.

"Wonderful, sweetheart. I'll send you the address as soon as we hang up," she says. "Really looking forward to finally meeting you. Wells has told me so much about you."

Her parting words catch me off guard, rendering me momentarily speechless. Wells has always told me his relationship with his mom is lukewarm on its best days and an ongoing improvement project on its worst.

After Viviette legally adopted Wells as an infant, Mary Claire was the very definition of an absentee parent. She missed his first birthday, a string of Christmases, and years' worth of milestones. She couldn't be bothered to stick around for any of it, not when she had a whole life waiting for her outside the "suffocating confines" of Westhaven. At least, that's what she told Viviette and that's what Viviette told Wells when he was old enough to start asking questions.

It wasn't until Wells's teenage years that Mary Claire began coming around more, wanting to establish some sort of relationship with him; a move that didn't go over well with the baby she abandoned; a baby who'd grown up to become a young man with feelings and opinions on the matter.

Their bond—if one can call it that—has been turbulent at times.

Radio silent at others.

And while they're currently on speaking terms, I'm sure Wells would have mentioned it if they were talking regularly and he was telling her "all about me."

I shake it off, chalking it up to a simple instance of exaggeration. My own mother does that all the time, curating her social media profile to make it seem like she visits her daughters in California more than once a year.

"Looking forward to meeting you, too," I say. A dull weight nags my middle. It seems wrong to meet her without Wells, but it is what it is and my book deadline grows more urgent with every passing day.

We end the call, and within seconds, a text comes through with an address to a coffee shop in Santa Monica called Steam West.

Flipping to a clean page in my notebook, I grab my pen and jot down the first dozen questions that come to mind, though I'm sure I'll come up with twice as many more once we start talking.

I collect my laptop and the rest of my items and head to my room to take a midmorning shower in hopes of making myself as alert and presentable as possible for our meeting later.

Twenty minutes later, I'm wrapped in a towel and poring over my half of the walk-in closet we share when something catches my eye outside my window. I glance for a second—at first, doing a double take when I realize it's Sylvie . . . and she's standing next to the pool.

The very pool where she had her accident.

With her gaze fixed on the tranquil water below, her sheer white robe ruffles in the breeze, tangling around her legs.

A moment later, Glenna rushes out of the cottage red-faced, huffing and puffing, a blur of lavender across the lush emerald lawn. Hooking her arm around Sylvie's narrow waist, Glenna ushers her back inside and the entire scene returns to the way it was: sparkling turquoise pool, carefully pruned bushes, abundance of colorful flowers, not a soul in sight.

In the nearly two months I've lived here, I've never seen Sylvie step foot outside her cottage—until now.

Was she trying to run away?

Is *that* what she wanted to tell me?

Either way, it has to mean something.

7

JADE

There's a photo of Mary Claire on Viviette's dresser, one taken in the late sixties or early seventies if I had to guess. She's standing in front of a sycamore tree sporting a red-and-blue-plaid pinafore, a crisp white turtleneck, shiny Mary Janes, curly pigtails the color of spun gold, and a toothless grin that stretches ear to ear.

I'm not sure what Mary Claire looks like these days, but I texted her a moment ago to let her know I got us a table and that I'm wearing a white T-shirt, light blue jeans, and a red patent leather headband. I wanted to look fresh and classic, not like I was trying too hard. While I can't imagine she's overly judgmental given her rebellious past, you only get once chance to make a first impression.

Wells said his mother got pregnant at a house party in Torrance the summer after her senior year of high school, that his father was an older boy she'd been crushing on for a while. According to Viviette, Mary Claire was over the moon about the pregnancy—until the boy of her dreams wanted nothing to do with it . . . or her.

The bells on the coffee shop door jangle, and I glance up from my phone and spot a woman with Viviette's same wavy, champagne-blonde mane and graceful, swanlike neck. Taking a spot at the end of the line, she slides her classic aviator sunglasses to the top of her head, letting her eyes adjust as she scans the chalkboard menu ahead. With cut-off blue jeans, a gold men's watch, and a chambray button-down cuffed at her elbows, she's the epitome of coastal cool.

The more I observe, the more I'm certain it's Mary Claire. I've seen enough Viviette Westmore movies to have memorized her mannerisms, her nuances, and her body language.

I clear my throat, straighten my pen and notebook, and pull up the recording app on my phone while I wait for her to notice me.

A few minutes later, she collects her drink from the end of the counter, and then she takes another glance around as she adds a sprinkle of cinnamon and a packet of Stevia to her mug.

Our eyes catch from across the room, and my heart does a somersault.

I knew from photos that she resembled her late mother, but I wasn't expecting a modern-day replication of the woman.

She's a piece of living history in the flesh, and while I never expected to be starstruck, I'm feeling as though a part of my soul has left my body.

Her pale pink mouth pulls up at the sides revealing a single deep dimple, and her blue gaze softens. Her excitement radiates from across the crowded coffee shop, and for a moment, I second-guess whether or not she's looking at me—or someone behind me.

She heads for my table, her long, toned legs taking confident strides as heads turn.

"Hello, hello! You must be the famous *Jade* I've been hearing all about." Her eyes light as she places her coffee down and greets me with arms open wide.

"I am." I hug her back, though I've never been a touchy-feely person.

"Oh, sweetheart." She lingers with me in a gardenia-coconut-sea-salt-scented embrace. "I can't tell you how wonderful it is to finally meet you."

Mary Claire rests her delicate, sun-kissed hands on my shoulders as she leans back and takes a better look at me.

"You're even lovelier than I imagined." She places a palm against her tawny décolletage before slinging her oversized designer bag over the back of her chair. "Wells told me you were pretty, but he didn't tell me you were a *dramatic ingenue*. My favorite of all the types . . ."

I attempt to maintain my fading smile. "Dramatic . . . ingenue?"

Tossing her head back, she chuckles and waves her hand, as if she's erasing the awkwardness she just laid on me.

"Wells hasn't told you what I do for a living, has he?" she asks.

"He has not . . ." In fact, he told me she was living with some investment banker who was footing the bill for her lifestyle—which I assumed meant she wasn't working.

"Have you ever heard of Kibbe body typing?"

"It sounds familiar . . ."

"I won't get into all the nitty-gritty, but basically women pay me to tell them what their body type is, and from there we narrow down their ideal silhouette and clothing style . . ." Her nose scrunches as she laughs. "Anyway, we didn't come here to talk business and I'm certainly not here to sell you on my services. Please, sit down, sit down. This is so exciting for me. I only wish my son were here to share this moment with us."

It's impossible to tell if she's being passive-aggressive or simply making a casual comment. Either way, the icy sting of embarrassment flushes through my veins. Wells should be here for this. I let my excitement for this meeting and my impending deadline get in front of my better judgment . . .

"I guess I was so excited to meet you, I didn't think about waiting another week for Wells to get home," I say. "Wife fail . . ."

She leans forward. "Oh, honey, no. That's not what I meant at all. I just never get to see him these days, and I was hoping to have met you by now. Anyway, I brought you something."

Digging into her oversized bag, she pulls out a gift-wrapped box hardly bigger than a set of playing cards.

"I didn't know we were exchanging gifts or I'd have brought you something . . ."

She slides it toward me, then gives it another nudge. "We're not exchanging gifts. You're a Westmore now. We have to make it official. Consider this your welcome gift."

With delicate precision, I tear the wrapping paper until a mahogany box is revealed. Uncocking the lid, I'm met with a gleaming gold locket in the shape of a heart.

"This is beautiful, Mary Claire. Thank you so much."

"Go ahead, open it up."

I slide my thumbnail into the opening along the side of the heart until it springs open, revealing an ornate engraved *W*.

Mary Claire tugs at the delicate gold chain hanging from her own neck until a matching gold heart pendant is revealed.

"I have the same one," she says before her eyes flinch at the corners. With a pained smile she adds, "As does Sylvie, of course."

"It's beautiful." I close the box and clutch it against my chest. "I can't wait to wear this."

"The original one was gifted to me from my mother on my sixteenth birthday—a replica of her favorite locket," she says. "Though if we're being honest, she shouldn't have gifted me anything that year. She didn't have it easy with me, that's for sure. I don't know if Wells has ever told you, but I was a little bit of a handful in my younger years."

I'm so glued to every word coming out of her mouth so far that I almost forget to hit record on my phone and hand her the clip-on microphone. Public interviews tend to be filled with background noise, but I've found an app that filters out the audible clutter.

"I'm sorry," she says as she watches me tap at my phone. "You probably want me to start at the beginning, right?"

"We can start wherever you'd like."

She takes the microphone from me and clips it on the lapel of her wafer-thin chambray blouse.

"You know I was adopted, right?" she says, using air quotes. If she's testing me to see if I've done my research, I can't be sure.

"Wells told me about that situation, yes. It must've been difficult for your mother to have to lie about that."

Mary Claire laughs. "Knowing her, it was probably the easiest thing she'd ever done. People think she was this ballbuster, but any time the studio told her to jump, she'd ask how high."

"Really?" I rest my elbow on the table, leaning closer. These are the kind of revelations I live for, the things that challenge decades of a carefully crafted persona.

"Validation was her Achilles' heel," she says. "The worst thing you could do to that woman was write her off or make her feel irrelevant. Believe me, I spent years exploiting the heck out of that when I was younger."

There's a humorous glint in her eye, as if a small part of her still gets a kick out of her teenage antics.

"I was awful to her," she adds. "I'll be the first person to admit that. She deserved better than what she got from me. But she wasn't perfect either."

"No one is."

She takes a sip, nodding. "Exactly."

"Wells says you never knew your father," I say. "It must have been hard for her, doing it all on her own."

"If by on her own, you mean with two full-time nannies and a household staff of five, then yes, she did it all on her own." Mary Claire winks. "Emotionally, though, yes. I think it was hard for her. Things could've been much worse, though. Plenty of women do the same thing without seven people on their payroll."

"Do you have any idea who he could be?" I get back to the million-dollar question, the one that's baffled cinematic history buffs for decades. "I know the rumor was it could've been a married costar?"

She shakes her head. "From what I've been told by people who were in her inner circle at the time . . . she was getting older, her success was waning, and she was desperate to make a comeback . . . she was *propositioned* by a powerful producer who promised her a role in one of his films . . . you can infer the rest."

I lean back, soaking it all in. "Wells never told me that part of the story."

"And he wouldn't." Her gaze falls to the table for a second. "My mother sheltered Wells from the real world, from anything that could remotely disappoint him. The versions of events she gave him were . . . watered down . . . and of course painted her in the most flattering colors. The woman knew her lights and angles, I'll give her that."

"Did she shelter him from it for his benefit . . . or for her own?" I ask.

"That's not even a debate." Mary Claire crosses her long legs before inching closer. "For herself, no question."

If everything Wells has shared with me so far about Viviette has been a manipulated version of the truth, my biography will be, too. I have no interest in publishing fictitious facts or intentionally "misremembered" stories.

"Wells doesn't describe her that way," I say. "At all."

"And again, he wouldn't. Self-serving aside, she was a loving mother to him. He had everything she could never give me—emotionally speaking, and he was all the things she wanted me to be and more. Docile. Disciplined. Devoted. Wells got the best parts of her. She was older, retired, never left the house. He gave her life purpose again. Gave her companionship. And he was a good kid. My God, he was perfect. And cute as a button. It worked out for both of them, I guess."

"Was it hard going home and seeing the two of them together?" I ask. "And their special bond?"

"Why do you think I quit coming around?" she asks with a sniff. "That's been a point of contention between Wells and myself over the years. He feels like I abandoned him, when really I saved him from me. The last thing he needed was my influence in his life."

"Excuse me, is anyone using this chair?" A young mother with a chubby toddler on her hip points to the extra seat at our table.

"Goodness, no, it's all yours," Mary Claire says before grinning and waving at the small child. "Do the two of you want children?"

"Oh, um . . ." It's not a straightforward answer, nor is this a question I was anticipating today.

"I'm sorry. I know it's a deeply personal question, and you don't owe me an answer." She places a hand over her heart locket, and her voice is whisper soft. "I just saw you looking at that little guy and I was curious. That and you're probably my last hope at having grandkids."

Probably.

Is it because I'm diving headfirst into my last remaining childbearing years? Or is it because she isn't sure we'll stand the test of time?

I refuse to let myself assume she's speaking out of malice or passive-aggressive behavior.

"Um, honestly, I've never been bitten by the motherhood bug," I say in a way that doesn't make me sound like a kid-hating thirtysomething woman. Not that I hate kids, but people like to make assumptions when you take the road less traveled in adulthood. I happen to love children—I just can't picture raising any of my own.

"I wasn't meant to be a mom," Mary Claire says, ignoring my confession. "But I'd be the best grandmother ever, I just know it. Would you have a baby for Wells? If he asked you to?"

Once again, I'm speechless. Not because I have nothing to say, but this time it's because I'm fighting back all the words I *want* to say.

"Wells said he could go either way," I say. "Between work and everything else, I don't know how we'd fit parenting into any of that."

"There are ways," she says with a wink that I assume means hired help. "I'd just hate to see our legacy die out."

Perhaps that's why Wells is so hell-bent on preserving Westmore, it's a way for his grandmother's legacy to live on without having to bring a child into a world rife with diseases, wars, climate change, social media, and human trafficking.

"I don't think Viviette's legacy could ever die out," I say. "She's a legend. Legends never die."

"Sylvie wanted a family," Mary Claire says with a sigh. "Before everything, of course. The woman loved children. Had such a knack with them. And homeless dogs. And senior citizens."

Her description of Sylvie reminds me of someone with a savior complex, a God-sized hole of guilt they're trying to fill with good deeds and karma points and things that make it easier to look in the mirror every day.

"She was as broken as she was beautiful, that girl," Mary Claire says. "Obsessed with saving the world one unwanted soul at a time."

"What do you mean?"

"Very difficult childhood. Bounced around from different foster homes. Finally got adopted by a wealthy family when she was in her teens. Almost overnight, she became one of those trust fund kids, the ones who treat nightlife like it's a full-time job, the ones famous for being famous. She was one of *those* . . ."

I'd seen her described in a couple of places as a socialite, but I never saw any mention of her adoption. They say adoption can be traumatic no matter the age of the child. I imagine a much younger Sylvie being passed from family to family, never feeling wanted or like she belonged somewhere. It's only fitting that she grew up trying to fit in as best as she could, looking for ways to be not only wanted, but needed, too—hence her charity.

"Have you met her yet?" Mary Claire asks.

I shake my head. I'd tell her about what happened yesterday morning, but I haven't even told my husband yet so it wouldn't be right.

"Wells thinks it might upset her," I say.

"Will it upset *her*? Or will it upset *him*?" She arches a slender brow.

"Not sure. Either way, he's not ready yet. He wants to take his time and do this right. There's no handbook for this sort of thing, you know?"

She rests an elbow on the table, inhales a long breath, and gazes out the window to her right. Traffic is backed up and the sidewalk is full of passersby walking dogs and pushing strollers and carrying oversized shopping bags.

"She was an interesting choice for him," she says. "He was always more of a loner, a classic introvert. Hated the social scene, hated going out, particular about who he spent his time with—complete opposite of me. But he went out one night for a close friend's birthday . . . and in walked *her* . . . this glamorous, outspoken party girl with more friends than she knew what to do with. He was taken from the moment he laid eyes on her . . . obviously she was a stunningly beautiful young woman. I just . . . they were night and day, those two. The whole opposites attract thing is fine and well when you're dating, but when it comes to marriage—it completely changes things, and not necessarily for the better."

"All relationships have peaks and valleys."

"Of course they do. There was just something about her that never sat right with me. Why would someone who jet-sets around the world making nightclub appearances want to all of a sudden throw it all away for a quiet life in the suburbs raising a soccer team of children?"

"Maybe deep down that's what she wanted? Maybe she was tired of partying? Maybe she thought she finally met The One and she was ready to settle down?"

"Sometimes I wonder if she simply took one look at him and saw the opportunity of a lifetime." Mary Claire shrugs, her tone particularly casual for a woman making pointed accusations about someone unable to speak up for themselves.

"I thought Wells proposed to her several times before she said yes? That doesn't sound like an opportunist to me."

"Oh, honey, playing hard to get is the oldest trick in the book," she says with an amused chuckle. "Men only want what they can't have, and Wells is no exception."

"I don't know about that . . ." I keep my voice light, so as not to come off as too contentious. But I vehemently disagree.

As things with Wells progressed in the romance department, I didn't throw myself at him, but I didn't play games either. He didn't strike me as the kind who appreciated a good cat-and-mouse hunt, and I certainly didn't want to turn him off by acting like I wasn't falling head over heels for him.

I wanted to screw *him* . . . not his head.

And the fun kind of screwing, at that.

"You know, Sylvie was engaged twice before Wells. Once to a plastic surgeon twice her age and another to some Italian shipping heir. She broke off both engagements just months before the weddings. Thought maybe she'd do the same with my son . . . Anyway, that's neither here nor there," she says. "I guess we'll never know what kind of mother Sylvie would have been. It's all very tragic, what happened. I'm just glad Wells was finally able to move on. For a while, I thought he'd spend the rest of his life taking care of her."

"Nothing wrong with that," I say. "I mean, they did make vows . . . *'til death do us part.*"

"They also made a pact," she counters without pause. "Which I imagine was all Wells's idea. He's never been good at being alone for too long."

"Really?"

Wells has never mentioned having any relationships after Sylvie's accident and before I came along. In fact, I got the impression his focus was solely on getting her the medical setup she needed, which required almost a solid year filled with various doctor appointments, flying around the world to visit specialists, and interviewing various visiting nursing agencies until he found the perfect one.

"I blame myself for his abandonment issues." She eyes her empty coffee mug. "A mother giving her child away, no matter the reason, no matter how wonderful the child's life turned out to be, that's got to sting deep down."

"You were just a kid . . ." I let my words fade. "If it's any consolation, he doesn't seem resentful at all when he talks about you."

Indifferent—but not resentful.

"No need for consoling, Jade, but thank you. We're in a better place these days." She folds her hands in her lap as her lips slink into a slow smile. "And by that, I mean I can call him and he doesn't send me to his voicemail every time." She chuckles. "I'm only half kidding, but yes, we're on the right track at least."

There's a hint of pain in her voice, one that isn't obscured by the pleasant expression she's wearing. I can't imagine how difficult it must have been to have a baby at nineteen with no help from the father. I'm sure she was terrified. And I can only assume Viviette was trying to do the right thing by adopting Wells.

Reaching for my pen, I clear my throat. "Do you mind if we switch gears a little? I'd like to go back to the beginning and talk about your childhood at Westhaven."

Mary Claire sits straight before recrossing her legs and settling into her chair. Slipping her french-manicured fingers through her hair, she tousles her blonde waves into place, like someone important about to be interviewed and wanting to look their best before the camera starts rolling.

"Of course," Mary Claire says as she straightens the collar of her blouse.

There's no denying from Viviette's diary entries that she was fixated—no, consumed—with her appearance at all times. Viviette's appearance was her currency, her moneymaker, and at times, her weapon. Dressed by the best international couturiers, styled by the greatest stylists, and dolled up by legendary makeup artists and hairdressers, Viviette was obsessed with presenting her best face to the world.

I imagine that sort of fixation trickles down when you have a child . . . particularly when you have a daughter. My own relationship with my mother isn't half as complicated as theirs, but there's no doubt insecurities can be passed down generationally, finding their way into fissures and cracks until they're buried so deep in our marrow they become second nature.

I check the recording app on my phone, ensuring that it's active, and then I press my pen against my notebook. I learned the hard way early on that all interviews should be documented twice: digitally and manually, for backup purposes.

"What's your earliest memory of your mother?" I ask.

Before Mary Claire can utter a single word, a phone call from Wells fills my screen, pausing the recording.

"Sorry about that," I say, silencing his call. "Wells is out of town for a project . . . he was probably just calling to tell me about his day."

"You should take the call," she says in a way that feels more like instructions than a courtesy.

"All right," I say, intending to tell him I'll call him as soon as I leave here. I tap the green button and lift the phone to my ear. "Hey . . ."

"Thank God you answered." He exhales into his receiver.

"Everything okay?"

"No," he says without hesitation. "Are you home? You're not, are you?"

"I'm actually having coffee with Mary Claire in Santa Monica." I use her given name since that's what Wells does. "We were just about to go over some questions for the book. What's . . . going on?"

"I hate to ask," he says, "but I just got a call from Sylvie's nurse. She slipped out of the guesthouse when the nurse was in the bathroom and she can't find her anywhere. Would you mind running home?"

"Did she check the main house?" I ask.

Mary Claire lifts a brow as she listens to my half of the conversation.

"It's locked," he says. "But it's possible Sylvie got in through the side door—the lock with the fingerprint scanner . . . I don't know what she'd be doing in there or why she'd want to go in, but—"

"I'll leave right now and see if she's there." I don't hesitate. In fact, I'm already up out of my chair and slinging my bag over my shoulder.

"I'm so sorry to involve you in this," he says.

"Don't be. I've got it," I say.

"Call me when you get home . . . let me know either way," he says before we hang up.

"I hate to cut this short," I tell Mary Claire. "But apparently Sylvie has wandered off and I need to help find her."

The strangeness of speaking about a missing woman the same way one might speak about a house cat who slipped out the back door isn't lost on me.

"Oh, no." Mary Claire's rosy lips part as her jaw turns slack. "Do you need any help?"

I'd hate to make her drive down Wilshire this time of day, given that it was the whole reason why she chose this coffee shop out of the dozens upon dozens in the area. I'd also hate to make her spend her evening searching for someone she was essentially referring to as an opportunist mere moments ago.

"I don't think so," I say. "Thank you, though. Maybe we can pick this back up tomorrow?"

I check my watch. It's almost five, which means sitting in bumper-to-bumper traffic the whole way home. Time is of the essence, but there's nothing I can do but cross my fingers and hope for an abundance of green lights.

"Absolutely, I'd love that," she says as she rises from her chair. Tucking a glossy lock of golden hair behind one ear, she steps toward me. "Can I tell you something . . . off the record? Mother-in-law to daughter-in-law?"

"Of course."

"There's something special about you, Jade." She gathers my hands in hers and anchors me with a disarming gaze the color of a still blue sea. "I can already tell you're a keeper."

8

JADE

Aside from the hum of the fridge and the ticking of the grandfather clock in the study, the house is too quiet when I arrive home. Any and all staff have long since gone home. The sun's already going down, but inside it might as well be night. All lights are off, all curtains are pulled closed, all signs of life are nonexistent.

Sylvie's nurse, Glenna, all but sprinted to me the second I pulled up, wearing the frantic mask of someone more worried about losing their job than the safety status of her charge. As I fumbled with the door lock, she rambled on about how she'd only *walked into the other room for a second and nothing like this has ever happened in her twenty-nine years of being a nurse.* I was too concerned about getting inside than listening to her excuses, so I didn't waste my breath telling her she was barking up the wrong tree. It's Wells she'll have to take that up with, and while he's generally a rational and forgiving soul, I don't know what he'd do if something happened to Sylvie . . . again.

"Hello?" I call out from the foyer. My voice echoes against the tall ceilings.

No response.

"You take the main floor, and I'll go upstairs," I tell Glenna.

I called Wells on the drive home to ask if he wanted me to alert the authorities about her unknown whereabouts, but he'd just finished reviewing the security camera footage which confirmed that she was, indeed, inside the main house. Only when he attempted to pull up the interior cameras, half of them were offline—an issue that's normally fixed by a hard reboot of the mainframe at home. With all of his staff gone for the day, there was no one to physically pull the plug.

Each passing minute felt like an endless loop as my car crawled along sunbaked asphalt with a million other cars.

I couldn't get here fast enough.

With my heart in my throat, I climb the sweeping staircase, my hand trembling as it glides up the cold metal rail. When I get to the top landing and spot our bedroom door ajar, I stop. I know I closed it when I left—I always do.

"Hello?" I call out again. "Sylvie? It's . . . Jade."

The muted shuffle of footprints against plush carpet sends my stomach to the floor.

She's in our bedroom.

I give the double doors a push, until they're all the way open, and then I reach in to flick on the lights.

"Oh, my God." I clamp my hand over my mouth as I comprehend the disaster waiting for me. Heirloom lamps tipped over. Antique paintings ripped off walls. The bedding torn from the mattress. Dresser drawers overturned, their contents dumped on the floor.

Either she was looking for something—or looking to send a message.

Maneuvering through the mess, I head to the closet where a light illuminates the underside of the door and the hollow rattling of wooden hangers bumping against each other waits for me.

"Sylvie?" I wrap my hand around the knob and take a deep breath. "Sylvie, it's Jade. I'm coming in."

Giving the door a gentle push, it swings a couple of feet before I'm met with resistance. Peeking in, I steel myself when I spot all of my clothes in countless heaps on the floor.

None of Wells's items are among the mess.

Only mine.

On the other side of the door, Sylvie sits cross-legged on the carpet, staring ahead at the empty closet wall where my things hung moments ago. There's no life in her eyes. No heavy breathing to indicate she was recently worked up. I'm not sure how long she's been sitting here like this.

"Glenna, I found her," I call.

Sylvie doesn't move, doesn't stir, doesn't blink.

Doesn't acknowledge my presence.

In an instant, Glenna rushes in, squeezing past me.

"Sylvie, my goodness," Glenna coos. "What on earth are you doing in here? Are you okay? Let me help you up, sweetheart."

She speaks to Sylvie like she's a preschooler who fell on the playground, rather than a heartbroken woman trying to process the fact that her former husband moved on without warning.

Sliding her hands under Sylvie's arms, Glenna helps her stand before looping her arm around Sylvie's narrow waist and leading her through the bedroom and into the hall. She doesn't look at me in passing.

I follow them, keeping a careful distance between us if only because I imagine Sylvie wants nothing to do with me at the moment.

I won't pretend to be a hero in a situation where all I did was unlock a door.

"Let's get you back home, Sylvie," Glenna says as she helps her down the curved stairs to the Saltillo tile foyer—the very floor she once walked as the first Mrs. Westmore, when her entire life was still ahead of her. "I'll draw you a nice bath, how about that? And I'll make you some chamomile tea. You've had quite the eventful little evening. I think maybe you ought to turn in early tonight. Get some good rest."

The grandfather clock reads half past six.

Not only does Glenna speak to Sylvie like a child, she's giving her a child's bedtime.

I wait until they're gone and quietude falls over the house before calling Wells.

"Found her in our room," I say when he answers in the middle of the first ring.

"What?" he asks. "H—how . . . why?"

I rest against the closet doorframe, feasting my gaze on the work that lies ahead. And I imagine him pacing, his fingers ruffling his thick dark hair as worry lines spread across his forehead.

"She . . . um . . . she trashed it." Dropping to my knees, I gather clothes in my arms and carry them to the bed to sort through everything. Phone cradled on my shoulder, I begin making piles. Dresses. Jeans. Sweaters. Blouses. "Well, my stuff. Not yours. She left all of your things alone."

His silence is unnerving, though it isn't out of character for him. He's generally a man of few words, but in this instance I wish he'd say *something*.

"I . . . uh," I start to say, "the other day when the nurse left . . . she asked me to help with Sylvie until the replacement came. I went to the guesthouse and—"

"I know."

I place the ivory linen skirt in my hands aside and take a seat on the edge of the bed.

"I should have told you sooner," I say. "I'm so sorry, I didn't want her to be alone in case anything happened and you're on the other side of the country . . ."

"Jade, it's fine."

I exhale, feeling silly.

Of course it's fine.

Wells is a sensible, understanding man.

Then again, why didn't he bring it up if he knew? Was he waiting for me to bring it up first? Or was it simply . . . not a big deal?

"She saw the ring on my finger," I say. "And judging by the state of our bedroom, it's safe to say she knows you've moved on."

"Yeah." My husband sighs, and I picture him folded over in the darkness of an icy hotel room, his elbows on his knees as he pinches the bridge of his aquiline nose. "How are you? You doing okay?"

"I'm all right. I just feel awful . . . for the both of you. I hate that she's upset, and I hate that this is all happening when you're away. You already have enough going on."

"Her doctor's beeping in, Jade. I'm so sorry—I need to let you go," he says.

"Of course."

"I love you," he says the words that always punctuate the end of our phone calls.

"I love you, too." I return to my mountains of clothing, carrying them to the closet and placing them on hangers, one by one, until the space looks the way it did before Sylvie went unglued.

I head to the bathroom next, only one step in and I'm met with the crunch of shattered glass beneath my shoe. My stomach sinking, I flick on the light and scan the mess waiting for me.

Fragmented powders and spilled foundations leave earth-toned smears against the bright turquoise floor tiles, and all of my perfume bottles are shattered. My vanity drawers are yanked out, nearly dangling off their tracks. The space smells like the perfume section of a department store with its jarring symphony of fragrances, and it looks like a coastal city after a hurricane.

Once again, only *my* things that have been destroyed—nothing of Wells's.

Crouching, I pick chunks of glass from the wreckage and place them carefully in my cupped hand. Next, I wipe up the spilled lakes of perfumes and rivers of foundations with a nearby towel, scrubbing the off-white grout as best I can.

I can't imagine what she'd have done had I been home . . . or maybe I don't want to.

Wells told me that after their marriage ended, he insisted on keeping her near to monitor her care, but the doctors said it would be too confusing for Sylvie to go back and forth to the house where she once lived. After an in-depth meeting, they all decided giving her a consistent routine and keeping her in the cottage would be the least taxing on her emotionally. It would also be a way to help her understand that while Wells was still a part of her life, he was no longer her spouse.

Many times I've imagined what I'd have done in Wells's shoes, and it always shakes out the same. He has the wealth and means and space to keep her close and well cared for. Not to mention the guilt he'd feel for sending her to some long-term care facility where she'd be out of sight, out of mind. I don't blame him at all for this unconventional setup, for paving his own road. If anything, it's a move that quietly commands respect.

There's got to be a way to make this work without upsetting Sylvie again.

I carry the broken glass to the trash can under the sink—only when I get there, I find another message waiting for me. This time, it's written in pale pink lipstick on the mirror—hence why I didn't notice it until now.

That message? *Run.*

9
JADE

"Liar," Portia mumbles as her manicured fingers tap out a furious text. Gathering a stiff breath, she lets it go before placing her phone face down on her kitchen island and returning her attention to me. A smile replaces the scowl that resided on her perfectly symmetrical face mere seconds ago. "Sorry about that. I made dinner reservations for tonight and lined up a babysitter so my husband and I can celebrate our ninth wedding anniversary . . . but apparently he has other plans. You ever love someone and hate them at the same time?"

I was three all-new chapters into my manuscript earlier today when Portia asked if I wanted to take a walk with her and Lily. She said she was craving the company of another adult, and I was in desperate need of some fresh air. After meandering around the neighborhood as she filled me in on everyone's fortune, fame, scandals, and personal tragedies, we somehow ended up back at her place splitting an afternoon bottle of Riesling.

"I'm so sorry, can't say that I have." I cock my head in sympathy. "That must be so frustrating."

She swats a hand, takes a sip of her wine, and rolls her eyes. "Don't be. I know *what* I married. I know *whom* I married. I signed up for this in front of six hundred wedding guests, in head-to-toe Versace, thinking

I had it made." Portia sniffs. "God, I was a smug idiot back then. Truly. I cringe when I think about the woman I used to be. Funny how much a marriage can change a person, isn't it? For better—and for worse."

I can't begin to comprehend Portia and all of her complexities and idiosyncratic behaviors, but I can appreciate her straightforward style. Over the past hour, not only has she given me the name of the woman who does her lips, she also confessed to using a nanny cam to catch her husband in the act with the night nurse they hired when Lily was first born. That conversation somehow morphed into one about getting her vagina tightened via some laser procedure and subsequently giving her "second" virginity to some young Italian businessman she met at a club instead of her husband (out of sheer spite).

We both agreed the punishment fit the crime.

"Sometimes I think he gets off on being an asshole," she says, taking another swill of pale gold liquid. "Like I can just picture him choking his fat little dick in his office as he thinks about me sitting at home pissed off. Not that I'm pissed. I'm not giving him that."

The visual of some faceless middle-aged man jerking himself off in his office makes me chuckle so hard, I nearly snort wine through my nose.

"I'm sorry," she says in a way that makes me believe she is wholeheartedly not sorry. "You probably didn't need to know that."

No topic is off-limits with Portia—which is fast becoming my favorite thing about her.

"I just want to know how you keep a sense of humor about all of this," I say.

"It's pretty much my superpower." She winks before topping off her wineglass. As soon as we got back from our walk, she laid Lily down for a nap and said we had a solid two hours to relax before Lily's predinner witching hour began—which works out perfectly since Mary Claire is stopping by later this afternoon so we can finish our interview.

"Can I ask you something random?" I preface my question, knowing it isn't random at all. It's one of the reasons I jumped at the chance to spend time with Portia again after last night's incident with Sylvie.

"Anything." She leans closer, her elbows gliding against her immaculately polished countertop.

"When Wells and Sylvie were married . . . did she ever strike you as jealous?" I bite my lip and wait for her response.

Portia's dark brows lift. *"Sylvie? Jealous?"*

She blows a puff of breath through pursed lips.

"There wasn't an ounce of envy anywhere on that woman," she said. "Sylvie was the epitome of confidence. Damn near wrote the book on it, and believe me, I took notes. If anything, Wells was the jealous one."

I lean back, attempting to digest that last tidbit. "Really . . ."

"You seem surprised," she says, a hint of amusement coloring her tone. I get the impression she wants to dig deeper into this. Fortunately for her, so do I.

"Yeah, he's just never been that way with me."

"Are you a flirt?" Before I can reply, she adds, "Sylvie was a flirt. I don't think it was intentional, it's just the way she was. Charming, you know? Could talk to anyone for five minutes and they'd walk away feeling like they'd known her for five years."

It's a stark, tragic contrast to the shell of a woman she is today.

"Men—sometimes women, too—were drawn to her like moths to flames," Portia continues. "I never blamed Wells for being possessive, for feeling like he had to keep her on a tight leash. She was magnetic."

"When you say he was possessive . . . what was that like? What did he do?" This is the second time Portia has brought up Wells's possessiveness to me. Now I'm desperate for her to paint me a Technicolor picture of a side of my husband I've never known.

"Oh, God. Let's see. Where do I even start?" She laughs, tossing her head back like this is humorous to her—then again, what isn't funny to this woman? "I need to remind myself it's your husband I'm talking about. I don't want to say something that might be offensive or upsetting . . ."

"It takes a lot to ruffle my feathers."

"You sure?" she asks, though I doubt my answer matters one way or another. I can tell by the twinkle in her dark irises that she's ready to spill all the tea. "Because people say that but seldom do they mean it."

I nod. "I mean it."

I was born with thick skin, and being in this city the past nearly fifteen years has only made it thicker. Besides, there's nothing someone could tell me about Wells that would change my perception of him. I love him for who he is today—not for who he was before I knew him.

"I told you about the curfew thing, right?"

"Right."

"Well before that incident, there was the time we had them over for a party one evening, and every time Sylvie had to use the restroom he'd walk her there, wait outside the door for her, and then walk her back. At first I thought he was just being an old-fashioned gentleman—having been raised by Viviette and all. But after the curfew thing and him knowing her phone passcode and all of that, it sort of stood out to me as something a possessive partner would do."

I rest my chin on the top of my hand, studying her face. Oftentimes women with the proverbial gift of gab also have the gift of embellishment. They tell a good story and they love to bedazzle it with dramatic details for effect.

But Portia doesn't strike me as someone who has the time to keep her stories straight, filtered, or edited. From what I can gather so far, she calls things like she sees them.

I'm about to ask my next question when my phone rings.

"I'm sorry," I say when I find Mary Claire's name flashing across my screen. "It's Wells's mother. We're supposed to be meeting this afternoon . . . I should take this." I tap the green button and press my phone to my ear. "Hello?"

"Jade, hi. It's Mary Claire," she says. "I was running a few errands in the area and happened to finish earlier than expected. Would you mind if I headed over now?"

I look at Portia, then to the bottle of wine resting between us. Our conversation was ripe for the picking, and now it's going to wither on the vine.

"Yes, of course," I tell Mary Claire. It wouldn't be right to make her wait. Family or no, I've learned over the years to treat my interviewees like gold. Their information is priceless, and so is their time.

"Wonderful. I'll see you at the house in a few. You'll need to buzz me in at the gate," she says before hanging up.

"I'm so sorry," I say to Portia as I rise from the white leather counter stool I'd just begun to settle into a moment ago. "She wants to do the interview now instead of later."

"No worries," Portia says, though judging by the fading smile on her face, she doesn't mean it. And I get it. We were having a moment. We were bonding. We were about to discuss a topic equally exciting to each of us but for our own reasons.

"If you're around later, maybe we can pick up where we left off?" I ask.

"Maybe," she says. "Since Lee ditched me, I might just take Olly and Lily out for dinner instead."

"There you go," I say. "I'm free tomorrow if you want another walking partner."

"I'd love that." She walks me to the door, and I'm down her driveway when I spot a sleek platinum Mercedes parked at the gate.

That was fast.

Trotting home, I greet Mary Claire and punch the gate code in. While she parks, I run inside to grab my notes in preparation for our continuation of yesterday's interrupted interview.

She's standing in the foyer when I find her next.

"I can't get over how nothing has changed," she says with a gasp. "And I mean *nothing*."

"When was the last time you were here?"

"I've visited often over the years," she says with a wave of her delicate hand. "It just never fails to amaze me how time stands still every time I walk through that front door. It's almost like *she's* still here. Like she never left." Her gaze floats to the top of the stairs. "Although, I haven't been in my childhood bedroom in decades. I wouldn't mind peeking in there . . . for old times' sake."

"Of course," I say, turning back and heading upstairs. I've been in her room a handful of times lately—for research purposes. But I never stayed long. There are no real personal effects in there. No photos, diaries, journals, or even a dusty, forgotten old yearbook. It's as if Viviette wiped the room clean of any indication Mary Claire had ever slept there.

A moment later we're standing side by side, feet sinking into the luxurious pink carpet that spreads from wall to wall before seeping into an enormous walk-in closet like a lush river. A white canopy bed anchors the far wall and in the corner is a glass curio cabinet filled with dead-eyed porcelain dolls in frilly pastel dresses. Near the window stands a full-sized carousel pony, its paint still as fresh and glossy after all these decades.

Mary Claire takes a seat on the edge of her mattress, her eyes turning glassy before she blinks away the forming tears.

"It's a beautiful space," I say, eyeing the ceramic knobs of her dresser painted with little red roses. "I can tell she put a lot of thought and effort into making it perfect."

"This room never felt like mine." She reaches for the gray plush duck resting against her pillow. "It always felt like a room in a dollhouse that my mother decorated to fit what she thought a little girl's room should look like. All the pink. All the lace. All the dolls."

For the first time, when I study Mary Claire, I don't see a rebellious teenage daughter or an absentee parent. I see her wounded inner child fighting for surface air after decades of suffocation.

Rising from the bed, she places the duck back against the pillow and makes her way to the window. Pulling the lace-paneled curtains aside, she takes in the view of the shady, flower-speckled backyard with its glistening pool.

"I thought maybe you'd use *this* room as your office," she says. "It has the best views of all the bedrooms—except Mother's, of course."

"I use the spare room next door to this," I say. "The one with the desk and the bookshelves."

Her nose wrinkles. "I'm not familiar with that room. She must have designed it after I moved out."

I'm almost positive she's correct. I vaguely remember Wells mentioning Viviette converting a bedroom into a study for him, but I play dumb. She's already emotional, and I'd hate for her to clam up before our interview gets off the ground.

"You want to see it?" I ask, hoping it'll cheer her up. It'll also give me a chance to show her all the research I've collected on her mother. I want to show her I'm passionate about this project, that I'm doing everything in my power to shed dignity on her enigmatic mother's legacy.

We make our way to my office next, and I give her the official tour—which takes all of three minutes—before she takes a seat at my desk and runs her hands along the polished mahogany top.

"Is it weird?" Mary Claire asks, gazing out the window with its unobstructed view of the guesthouse. "You living here while Sylvie lives in the backyard?"

She doesn't *live* in the "backyard."

She lives in the guesthouse on property grounds.

I don't correct her, though.

"I wouldn't call it weird," I say. "Different, maybe."

Reaching for the framed wedding photo next to my laptop, she brings it closer for inspection. I hold my breath, waiting for her to make a comment, only she says nothing. She simply places it back where she found it after a quick glance.

"We didn't invite anyone," I say, nodding toward the picture and answering a question she never asked. "It was just Wells and I and a priest on a cliff in Monaco."

Our wedding was nothing like the lavish affair Sylvie and Wells threw on this very property, but it was private and personal and perfect for us. It may sound silly, but I felt like a modern Grace Kelly with my bobbed blonde hair and my off-shoulder dress billowing in the breeze as we recited handwritten vows. There isn't a thing I'd have changed about that day.

"We talked about having a small reception when we got home," I say, "but life got busy and it never really panned out."

"You're exactly the kind of person he should have married the first time around." Her remark throws me for a loop. Just when I expected some underhanded remark about being left out, she goes and drops a strange little compliment instead.

It feels wrong to thank her for that, though. All things considered.

"Life is funny sometimes," I say. "Funny-strange, not funny–ha ha."

"Isn't that the truth." She reaches for the stack of journals beside my laptop, and while I'm screaming on the inside for her to use the nitrile gloves before touching the time-worn paper, I bite my tongue. Touching them once with bare hands won't disintegrate them. "I always loved her handwriting. I used to try and copy it, but it never looked quite right."

Mary Claire returns the journal to the pile.

"You mind if we go to my mother's bedroom next?" she asks, running her palms down the sides of her thighs.

"After you." I motion for the door and follow her down the hall until we end up in the doorway of Viviette's suite. "I've been spending a lot of time in here while I write this book, but I've left everything exactly the way I found it."

Mary Claire doesn't seem to pay my words much attention as she scans the expansive room with its velvet-fringed drapes, hand-painted wallpaper, and abundance of teal, pink, and gold.

"I was never allowed to step foot in here as a child," she says as she stands in awe of the space around us. "This was her sanctuary, her sacred space. Of course when she was gone, I'd come in here. Try on her dresses or sample her perfume. I'd jump on her bed because I was a spiteful little girl. Sometimes I wonder if I was just trying to feel closer to her. There was always something so distant about my mother. The only times I felt like I could crack her perfect veneer was when I made her upset. Maybe that's why I was so rebellious. I wanted to know that she cared."

"Did she care?"

"In her own way." Mary Claire makes her way to the gold-and-glass bar cart in the corner, one filled with Baccarat decanters and a glass still smudged with Viviette's dark pink lipstick. "I was nine when she told me she wished I were a boy. She wanted a boy, and she made that very clear more times than I could ever count. Though she never elaborated. Guess it's something that stuck with me all these years. I still think about it sometimes. Isn't that absurd? I'm sixty-four and I've never been able let that go."

She runs a finger over the lid of the first decanter before lifting it and bringing it to her nose.

"Ballinger's brandy," she says with a shudder. "My mother used to drink this like it was water. Straight, no chaser. I couldn't forget this smell if I tried. This and that god-awful perfume of hers . . . what was it . . . it was *minty* almost . . . made me think of mouthwash and men's aftershave."

"Florida Water?"

"Yes, that's it. Florida Water." She snaps her cherry-red manicured fingers. "She used to say if it was good enough for Lucille Ball, it was good enough for her. Never mind that she was pretty much the only person who didn't *love* Lucy. They had an interesting dynamic, those two. A bit of fire, a bit of ice. If you ask me, my mother was jealous of Lucy's gumption and all the attention she got for portraying the first interracial marriage on screen and the first pregnancy in a sitcom. Different times, and all of that." Mary Claire pauses, and a distant expression colors her face as she gazes off. "Not many people know this, but early in my mother's career, she fell in love with an Argentinian man who worked as an on-set dance coordinator for one of her musicals. As soon as her studio found out, they demanded she break it off. I don't think she ever got over him—or the fact that Lucy got away with it but she couldn't."

"Heartbreaking."

"She could have chosen him," she says, matter-of-fact. "She could have walked away from her career and married him and lived happily ever after. But she chose herself. My mother *always* chose herself."

With that, Mary Claire leaves the room, and we make our way around the rest of the second level before ending up in the suite I share with Wells.

"Does it bother you that this place hasn't changed a bit since before JFK was shot?" she asks with an amused sniff as she ambles around *our* sacred space. Reaching for a hobnail milk-glass vase on the chest of drawers, she straightens it ever so. "You're living in a museum. You know that, right? Does it feel like home or are you constantly worried you might break something?"

"I love it here." While breaking something would be beyond awful, I'm careful and considerate, not to mention grateful to be living under this iconic roof. If Wells has it his way, he and I will be the last people to ever inhabit Westhaven before it becomes a tourist attraction. It's an honor to respectfully share this space with him. "Some days I could pinch myself."

"One would hope so." She peeks her head into the en suite. An image from last night flashes through my mind. The smashed cosmetics. The lipstick on the mirror.

The warning.

I've cleaned it up enough so that no trace remains, but for some reason this morning, I couldn't bring myself to use the space. I've never given much credence to concepts like bad juju or negative energy, but something felt . . . off . . . or maybe a part of me felt violated. I got ready in one of the guest baths instead.

Questions about Sylvie dance on the tip of my tongue, but I swallow the words before they force their way out. This is not the place and now is not the time. I invited her here to discuss her childhood and her mother—not my husband's ex-wife.

"I always hated this room," she says, closing the bathroom door. "My grandmother lived with us for a time before she died. Did Wells tell you that? This was her room."

"He mentioned it once."

Her lips tug down at the corners. "Horrible, wretched woman. I don't normally speak ill of the dead, but she was a bitter, angry, lost soul. Hated the idea of being a grandmother, so she made me call her by her first name: Vivian. She and my mother had a complicated relationship."

Mary Claire stops by Wells's side of the bed, running her fingertips along a marble-framed photo of the two of us from our wedding day, though with her back toward me, I can't tell if she's smiling or simply taking it in.

"Complicated like how?" I ask. This is the first I've heard anything about Viviette's connection with Vivian being intricate, though most mothers and daughters have complex dynamics when you examine their relationship under a microscope. All Wells has shared is that she passed away long before he was born, and there was a photo album around here somewhere. That, and the woman had starred in a handful of silent films before falling pregnant with Viviette. He surmised that she had a hand in pushing Viviette into show business, but he wasn't 100 percent certain.

"My grandmother had more moods than there were days of the year," she says. "Every morning, the instant I smelled her coffee, I'd hide in my room until I heard her door close and her shower turn on. She and my mother used to get into screaming matches . . . saying horrible things to one another . . . my grandmother blamed my mother for ruining her career. My mother blamed my grandmother for ruining her childhood. Whenever I'd hear them get into it, I'd sprint to my room and put a record on just to drown them out. To this day, I'll never understand why my mother let her live with us."

I think of the blonde, pigtailed little girl in the school uniform seeking refuge in her frilly pink room and my heart breaks.

Mary Claire abandons the wedding photo and heads for the door.

"I'm sorry. I can't stand to be in here another minute," she says as we return to the hallway. She's slightly winded, as if the heaviness of old memories is stealing the oxygen from her lungs. "Anyway, I know that's your bedroom, so I don't mean to put a damper on anything. The room has a lovely view. And square footage for days."

"Don't apologize at all," I tell her as we walk. "I'm sure this house unearths all kinds of ancient feelings for you."

"That's putting it lightly," she says with a soft chuckle. "It wasn't all bad, though. I don't mean to sound like a Negative Nancy. I hope you're not getting that impression from me."

"Tell me some of the good things you remember about this place," I say as we head down to the foyer. "Any favorite memories?"

She stops, takes a hard breath, and her hand curls around the iron banister. "Oh. Sure. You want to hear about the Christmas parties? My mother was famous for her parties, but her Christmas soirees were to die for. Seemed like the whole city came to those. Of course, I was relegated to my room, but I'd sneak out and watch from the top of the stairs . . . I loved seeing the beautiful dresses and hearing the piano player and smelling the food. My goodness. The food. She never spared a single expense on catering. She'd donate leftovers to local homeless shelters, and they'd feast for days after her parties."

Again, my heart breaks for the little girl who simply wanted to be a part of her mother's world. Though I'm inclined to give Viviette the benefit of the doubt in this case—keeping a child away from an adult's party is a matter of safety.

"Nineteen sixty-eight's party was a doozy, though," she says, pointing back at me. "Some crazed lunatic jumped the gate and stormed past security. He had a handgun, though no one was hurt, thank goodness. He said he was my mother's number one fan, and he wanted a picture with her. Claimed he'd been writing her for years, though all of her fan mail went to her agency—she never saw any of it."

"I actually read an article about that once."

"Not surprised. It was the talk of the town for a while. Mother was humiliated. The man caused such a scene before they escorted him out." Mary Claire rolls her eyes. "God forbid one thing didn't go absolutely perfect. She lightened up a little when people started seeing the humor in it. I guess you can laugh about those things when no one gets hurt."

We wind up in the living room next, standing under its cathedral ceiling with its dark-stained beams and stucco fireplace.

"This room always seemed so drab to me," she says, "so much brown and beige. Have you seen pictures of the kitchen before Wells got his mitts on it?"

"He showed me some, yes."

"I know he'll never touch another room in this house, but I'd love to see what he'd do with this space if he could. He's always had such an eye for design. If creativity runs in our DNA, it skipped me."

Heading to the back door, she steps outside, trekking over pavers and between potted ferns and palms until she reaches the pool.

"This," she says as she drags a breath of warm air into her lungs. "This was my happy place." Mary Claire kicks off her white canvas shoes and wades into the ankle-deep waters of the first step. "When I was out here, nothing else mattered. Used to swim for hours and hours . . ."

Stooping, she scoops a palmful of warm water into her hands before letting it slip through her fingers. If age is nothing but a number, Mary Claire's childlike wonder in this moment is proof of that.

"Still keeping it piping hot, I see," she says. "My mother hated cold water. She used to say it shriveled her soul. If that isn't melodramatic, I don't know what is."

"Wells says the warm water is good for inflammation and circulation." I'm not an expert in these matters. "I just think it feels nice, especially at night, when the sun's gone down. It's like a warm hug."

Mary Claire perches along the tiled edge of the pool, keeping her feet buried in the water. As comfortable as she looks, I could see her spending the rest of the afternoon out here, so I do the same for the sake of continuing our interview.

"Sylvie was big into that sort of thing." She nods to the left, toward the guesthouse. "Health and wellness and holistic alternatives. Sunrise yoga. Meditation retreats. I always saw her as two sides of the same coin—one was this wild party girl. The other was someone desperate to feel whole and at peace."

"Desperate?"

"After her accident, there was an initial investigation. They tried to say Wells pushed her into the pool or something ridiculous like that. They ended up saying she accidentally slipped in and hit her head, but sometimes I think she might have jumped in on her own accord, you know? There was always something so *unsettling* about her. Like . . . like a distance behind her eyes when she smiled. She was there, but not all the way there, if you know what I mean."

I clear my throat as our conversation takes a sharp left turn. One minute we were talking about the health benefits of water and the next minute she's accusing my predecessor of attempting to end her own life.

"It must be hard for her," Mary Claire says. "For Sylvie. Must be hard watching you live her old life. I know I couldn't do it."

I'm not sure what her fixation is on this issue or what all I can say to get her to drop it.

"Wells says he's not sure what all she understands," I say, still opting to leave out the part about her trashing our bedroom yesterday. Given Mary Claire's clear distaste for Sylvie, I don't want to give her any more ammunition on the matter.

"You know, at first I was convinced she was faking the whole silent thing, and I told my son that," she says. "I can't tell you how many doctors Wells took her to who couldn't figure out what was going on. They'd run tests, they'd prescribe medications to treat various symptoms, but there were never any definitive answers. Only theories and guesses.

But who are any of us to question medical doctors and so-called experts? Every time I spoke up, he'd get so upset with me he'd screen my calls for days. Eventually I threw my hands up."

She clucks her tongue and shakes her head.

"I had to step back from all of it because it was beginning to take a toll on my relationship with Wells, and we'd already come so far. I didn't want to lose him a third time," she continues.

"A third time?"

She straightens her spine. "Shortly after Wells got married, Sylvie and I had a heated conversation, and the next thing I knew, Wells was cutting me out of his life. Not completely, but enough to be noticeable. It wasn't until her accident that he let me come around regularly again. He needed me." Her lips press flat before forming a bittersweet smile. "When I first had him, I thought I was going to feel loved for the first time in my life. But the thing about babies is . . . they don't love you. They can't. They can only need you. And I needed love back then more than anything else. But now . . . forty-plus years later, I'm realizing that sometimes feeling needed and feeling loved are sort of the same thing."

She wipes a thick tear from the corner of her eye.

"Ugh. Here I am getting emotional on a weekday afternoon," she says, a hint of disgust lacing her tone. "I usually try to save those feelings for Sunday nights."

"Sunday nights?"

"Oh, just an old Viviette-ism. She used to believe a person should hold it together all week, then let it all out Sunday night, before the start of another week. Something about the build-up intensifying the release and going into the new week feeling lighter."

"That's fascinating." I glance down at my phone, ensuring it's still recording our conversation. "She referenced her 'emotional Sunday nights' in some of her diaries and now I have context."

We're heading back from the rose garden twenty minutes later when I spot an unfamiliar-looking nurse in pink scrubs entering Sylvie's house. A few seconds later, Glenna leaves. If Mary Claire weren't here, I'd use this as an opportunity to introduce myself to her and simultaneously check on Sylvie. But I don't want to leave Mary Claire hanging when she came all the way here for this interview—an interview I very much need in order to finish my manuscript.

"Let's head back in," she says, leading the charge to the back sliding door. "It's getting a bit buggy out, and I'm a mosquito magnet . . ."

With each passing minute, it becomes more apparent that Mary Claire is having the time of her life discussing herself—as many people do. The context she's given and the stories she has shared so far have been invaluable, and will make for some engaging chapters in Viviette's biography. But as Wells's mother rambles on, my mind is stuck on Sylvie.

"If you can think of any other questions, let me know. I'm just a phone call away," Mary Claire says a few hours later as I walk her to her car. She stops when she reaches the driver's door. With one hand splayed above her heart, she turns to me. "Jade, I have to say, this was such a lovely afternoon. I truly enjoyed our time, and I'd be honored to make this a regular thing."

"Of course," I say. "I'd love that."

"You know . . . I have a lot of regrets with Sylvie." Her lips press into a hard line and she pauses. "I made a lot of mistakes. Mistakes I won't repeat this time around."

With that, she leans in to kiss each of my cheeks before climbing into her Mercedes and leaving me in a billowing cloud of her expensive perfume.

I wait for her car to disappear past the gate before making a beeline to the guesthouse.

10

JADE

"Hi," I say to the nurse in pink scrubs when she answers the door. "I'm Jade . . . Wells's wife. Wells is out of town this week, so I just wanted to introduce myself."

Her name tag identifies her as Mackenzie, and her doe eyes and baby face suggest she's likely fresh out of nursing school. If Wells were here, he wouldn't be thrilled about this, especially since I've overheard him on the phone with Visiting Nurses requesting only "seasoned" nurses.

"Okay," she says with a shrug that tells me she's only here for a paycheck. Her phone chimes in the background.

At least I assume it's hers.

I can't imagine Sylvie has one—and if she did, I can't imagine who'd be texting her when she isn't capable of responding.

"Mind if I come in and check on Sylvie?" I ask, shamelessly preying on her inexperience in this position.

"Um, sure." She steps aside, and I make my way in.

The kitchen is spotless, as per usual. And Sylvie's bedroom door is propped open a few inches. I glance into the living room, where a flickering TV plays a late afternoon game show, but no one's watching it. Her chair is empty.

"Where is she?" I ask Mackenzie.

The flush of a toilet down the hall answers my question before she does.

"She doesn't need help in there?" I ask.

Mackenzie points to the black binder on the kitchen table. "It didn't say anything about bathroom assistance . . ."

She heads to the binder and begins frantically paging through it.

The sound of the bathroom faucet running comes next. I picture Sylvie ambling down the hall in a minute, taking one look at me, and freaking out in front of Mackenzie, who won't know what to do but will definitely make a note of it in the nurses' logbook, I'm certain.

I make an executive decision to intercept Sylvie before any of that has a chance to happen.

"I'm just going to see if she needs anything," I say before the nurse can protest. With my heart in my teeth, I head to the bathroom door and give it three light raps. In my calmest, softest voice, I say, "Sylvie, it's Jade."

The faucet stops running.

"I was hoping you'd have a moment to . . ." My words trail off as I realize I can't ask her to talk given the fact that she can't. "I just wanted . . ."

The door swings open. Sylvie stands before me with an unreadable expression and vacant eyes. This isn't the face of a madwoman tearing through my things.

"Hi," I say now that we're face to face. A gentle smile spreads across my mouth. I need to be delicate with her and respect the fragility of this situation. "I hope you don't mind me coming here . . . I just wanted to apologize for upsetting you the other day. And I'm sorry you had to find out about Wells the way you did. I'd have been angry, too."

There's no way to know how much of this she's comprehending.

Lowering my voice, I continue, "I know it's difficult for you to communicate."

More like impossible . . .

"But you wrote me a note." I lean in. It may have only been a single word, but it was a message regardless. "Not once, Sylvie. Twice."

She blinks, her arms limp at her sides and her stringy mud-brown hair framing her face.

"Are you . . . can you . . ." I clear my throat and try again. "Are you asking me for help? Or are you telling *me* to run?"

I wait in an endless moment of sheer silence, for an answer that doesn't come.

Before I get a chance to say another word, her lifeless eyes skim past my shoulder.

"Everything okay here?" Mackenzie asks, her gaze passing from Sylvie to me and back.

"Yeah," I say. "All good."

Mackenzie lifts an orange-brown pill bottle, giving it a couple of shakes. "It's five o'clock, Sylvie. Time for your lozepetrine."

The opportunity is over—if one can even call it that.

"I'll get out of your hair," I say, giving both women a gracious nod and squeezing past Mackenzie in the narrow hallway outside the bathroom.

Maybe it's all in my head, but I swear I feel the weight of Sylvie's stare pinning me in the back with each step I take to the door.

11

JADE

I'm standing in front of a humming microwave, heating a frozen dinner, when Wells calls.

"Good news," he says. "We made a lot of progress today, client signed off on moving forward, and I'm flying back first thing tomorrow morning."

My stomach does a mini somersault as my timer goes off. "Wells, that's great! What a nice surprise . . ."

I remove my organic chickpea rigatoni turkey Bolognese and place it on the counter to cool. Before he left, he gave his chef the week off, but not before requesting that he whip up a week's worth of nutritious, single-serve meals for my convenience.

"How's the book coming?" he asks.

After spending the afternoon with Mary Claire and attempting to have some miraculous breakthrough moment with Sylvie, it's been impossible to get focused, and I haven't been in the writing mindset.

"It's coming . . . slowly." I stir my pasta with a fork and blow the steam off the top. "Mary Claire had some interesting stories today."

He sniffs. "I'm sure she did."

"Learned a lot about your grandmother *and* her mother."

"Ah, the old two-for-one special," he teases. The lightness in his voice puts me at ease. Getting the green light from a demanding and high-profile client must take a load off. "I never knew Vivian. She passed before I came along. My grandmother never spoke of her much."

After the things Mary Claire shared today, I don't blame her. I'm sure her death was a much-needed reprieve. The closing line of a long chapter. The end of an era.

Anything Wells doesn't know yet, he'll know as soon as he reads my completed rough draft—whenever that will be.

"Oh, I asked the housekeeper if she knew where those journals might be," I say, while I'm thinking about it. "She said she's never moved anything out of Viviette's bedroom."

"So they must be in there somewhere," he says. "I'll help you find them when I get home."

"That'd be great—it's just so weird that they're not all together. Like someone had to have moved them at some point. Makes me think there's something juicy in them . . ."

Wells chuckles. "I hope for your sake you're not disappointed when we finally find them. Anyway, I'm going to order room service and get to bed."

A quick glance at the clock tells me it's already eleven PM there.

"Flight leaves at six," he adds, as if he read my mind, though it isn't the first time and surely won't be the last. Wells's intensity is only rivaled by his ability to read between the lines, to be one step ahead of everyone, and anticipate their every need.

Some would argue it's a trauma response, though from what I can tell, Wells's childhood was pretty damn idyllic by most people's standards.

"I won't keep you," I say.

"I love you."

"I love you, too." I end the call and eat my dinner over the sink, watching out the window as the sun dips in the sky and the guesthouse prepares for its nightly routine of curtains drawn closed and gentle lamps lighting the darkness.

I never knew it was possible for a home to look both cozy and desolate at the same time.

As soon as Wells is home tomorrow, my chances of talking to Sylvie without him knowing will be virtually nonexistent.

If I'm going to get answers, I won't be able to do this alone.

Waking my phone screen, I pull up my contacts and scroll until I arrive at Portia's name. She answers on the first ring, her greeting both chipper and casually desperate at the same time.

Ten minutes later, Portia is speechless, which I'm positive by now is no easy feat for her.

I check my phone screen, ensuring she's still there, that I wasn't playing to an empty room.

"It's not that I don't believe you," she finally says after digesting everything I've filled her in on thus far. "It's just that I didn't think it was possible for Sylvie to communicate . . . at least not based on what I've heard. It's just—"

"I know," I say. "Same. But it happened. Just wish I knew what it meant."

Portia exhales into the phone. "Give me twenty minutes to put Lily down for the night and then head over, okay? And bring wine. Or vodka. I'm all out at the moment and we're going to need it. You and me both."

My mind races a million miles a second as I run through various scenarios, questioning what Portia knows that she hasn't yet shared. "See you soon."

The line goes dead.

I check the time before slipping on a pair of sneakers.

The twenty minutes that follow are sheer torture.

12

JADE

"I promised I'd *never* repeat this." Portia is hunched over her pearly marble island, swirling a glass half full with the merlot I brought over a few minutes ago.

Her gaze is focused out the window behind me, staring into the abyss of her lush backyard with its shady palms, glimmering pool, and ripe citrus trees.

"And maybe that seems silly given everything that's happened since she shared this with me," she says. "Maybe it's irrelevant and I'm working myself up for nothing."

I lean closer, clinging on the edge of each and every word that leaves Portia's lips, only before she utters another syllable, a door down the hallway slams shut.

"Olly," she yells over her shoulder. "No slamming doors, Lily's asleep."

She stands in silence, ears perked like she's waiting for a response that never comes.

"Sorry," Portia says with an annoyed sigh. "He's been in a mood lately. And he gets weird when people he doesn't know come over. I mean, he's met you, but he doesn't know you yet. Just give him a little time and he'll come around. God willing."

Rolling her eyes, she buries her nose in her wineglass.

"Anyway, it feels wrong, telling you this." Portia places her drink down before massaging her temples. Dragging her fingers through her hair, she releases a soft groan. "Sylvie was thinking about leaving him. Wells. She wanted out. Their marriage was pretty much over. She told me the day before her accident and she made me swear I would never tell anyone because she wasn't 100 percent sure."

"Wait, wait, wait," I say, lifting a flattened palm. "So you're telling me she told you she was thinking of leaving Wells and the very next day she almost died? And you never told anyone this until right now?"

Portia offers an apologetic shrug, her loose cashmere cardigan sliding off her bare shoulder. "She told me I was the only one who knew that she was even *thinking* about leaving . . . and I know how much Wells loved her. I saw it firsthand. He would've never done anything to hurt her. Physically I mean. He might be a lot of things, but he's not that."

"And you know that how? Because you saw what went on behind closed doors?" I can't believe I'm asking this question in the context of my own husband, that I even have to question his involvement in any of this, but Portia's bombshell leaves me no choice.

There's an unspoken implication here.

"You said he was possessive and controlling," I say.

"Yeah, but he never hurt her or anything," she says. "I never saw any marks." Coming around the island, closer to me, she adds, "I know how I sound. Trust me. I get it. I sound like the idiot witness on some cable TV show. But I'm telling you, Wells adored her. He worshipped her. She was his oxygen. He would've been devastated about her leaving, but he wouldn't have killed her. He's a good man. You know it. I know it."

I also know that a person can think they know someone and end up knowing nothing about them at all.

13
JADE

Standing at the kitchen sink rinsing my tea mug the next afternoon, I suck in a startled breath as two cold hands snake around me from behind. Turning, I find my husband, his sandy-brown hair disheveled from a day of traveling.

I hadn't heard him come home.

He steals a kiss before I have a chance to properly greet him, curling his hand around my jaw and sliding his fingers through my hair.

His mouth against mine feels different today; almost like kissing a stranger who looks an awful lot like someone I used to know.

"God, I missed you," he says when he comes up for air. Brushing the hair from my forehead, he gazes down at me, drinking me in as a slow smile spreads across his handsome face. All my life, I always thought weak-in-the-knees was just an expression—until he came along.

Only today, there's nothing weak about me.

I stare back at Wells, studying his chiseled features and the disarming intensity of his ethereal hazel gaze—a familiar set of eyes that couldn't possibly belong to a possessive, controlling, violent version of the man I married.

I spent all last night tossing and turning, analyzing my entire relationship with Wells up until this point in search of red flags and warning signs that he wasn't who he claimed to be—only to come up empty-handed.

He's been nothing short of perfect from the instant we met.

In this moment, I think of Sylvie and the possibility that she was leaving him when her accident happened. And then I think of Mary Claire and her admission that Wells wasn't good at being alone. Lastly, my thoughts settle on the two of us . . . how he fast-tracked our relationship like he was in some sort of rush to seal the deal and make me his.

Did he love me?

Or did he simply not want to be alone another day more?

He kisses me again, this time a little longer, a little harder—almost as if he senses some emotional distance between us and needs to compensate for that.

Eyes closed tight, I kiss him back and say a silent prayer to anyone who's listening, and then I beg them to prove me wrong about him.

PART II
THREE YEARS AGO

14

SYLVIE

The white sheet of paper on my windshield flaps in the breeze, anchored only by a single wiper. I stop in my tracks, like I always do when this happens. From this end of the parking lot, I already know it isn't a flyer for some new pizza place or mobile car-detailing service. Those are typically printed on colors so bright they burn your retinas if you stare at them for too long. This one is the color of undriven snow and folded neatly in half.

Clutching my phone and keys like they're my lifeline, I make my way to my car, pluck the note off my windshield, stuff it inside my gym bag, and climb into the driver's seat. I jerk the car door shut and hit the lock button.

A cursory glance around offers no new clues as to who this person could possibly be—not that I'm surprised.

They're careful.

Discreet.

They don't want to be caught . . . they simply want me to know they're watching.

We're going on nearly a year of this now and there's been no relenting.

A group of young women wearing skintight yoga pants and coordinating neon crop tops climb out of the silver G-Wagon next to me. With rolled PVC mats tucked under their arms and ponytails bouncing, they make their way to the fitness center I just exited. For a moment, I debate calling out to them, asking if they happened to see anything. But they disappear inside before I get the chance.

It likely wouldn't have mattered anyway.

Anytime we've managed to capture my stalker on film, the details are always the same: slouched posture, baggy clothes, dark hat, chin tucked low. We've yet to see a face or determine a gender.

It could, quite literally, be anyone.

I drive home to my husband with my trembling hands gripping the steering wheel at ten and two. The cardio endorphins that were coursing through me mere moments ago have been replaced with molten-hot adrenaline.

I'm almost to Westhaven when a red light puts the brakes on my racing thoughts. I take the opportunity to gather in a long hard breath and some generous sips of water that cool me from the inside out, dousing the flames of my anxiety.

The first time this happened, Wells called out from work for a week, spending his invaluable office hours calling local police departments, three-letter agencies, and a slew of private investigators. This isn't his first rodeo. He's had stalkers in the past. But none of them have targeted his significant other. In fact, in this particular situation, the perpetrator only bothers me.

Never him.

The thing about Los Angeles is there's no shortage of creeps. I learned early on when I moved here years ago that the city attracts a certain kind of desperate, hopeless soul. Not unlike myself . . . before I met Wells.

By the time I pull up to our gate and enter the six-digit code, I'm debating on whether or not to tell Wells about this incident. He's already insisted on placing Bluetooth luggage trackers in and on all of my possessions should someone try and steal something personal of mine—or worse . . . me.

Just last month, he changed the settings on the security system so he's alerted via text any time there's activity of any kind. And he set it to the most sensitive setting so he's notified if so much as a sparrow flies past. Between the housekeepers, groundskeeper, chef, laundress, and myself, he must be receiving a hundred notifications a day.

Wells claims it doesn't bother him, that peace of mind is priceless and paramount.

Only the more peace of mind my husband gets, the more my freedom fades into distant memories.

I park inside the third garage stall, next to Wells's grandmother's 1955 Porsche 356, the silver one her character famously drove in the movie *To Hell and Back*. It's covered in beige canvas, mostly, save for its pitch-black tires with their shiny chrome wheel covers peeking out—tires yet to touch pavement since I've been around.

When we first started dating, Wells promised he'd take me for a ride in it sometime, painting a beautiful picture of the two of us cruising down the Pacific Coast Highway, the wind in our hair and the sun on our faces—like a scene from a golden-age film.

But life got busy, as it tends to do. My charity started taking off and Wells was tapped to lead a new project at work. Romance consisted of dinners at home and nights in bed.

I never brought the car up again, and it never bothered me all that much . . . until lately. Perhaps it's the fact that I'm home more—at Wells's request. When a person spends a disproportionate amount of time at home, she tends to notice more things: the drawer that sticks, the loose thread in the stair carpet, the way the groundskeeper sneaks in a daily nap around two PM behind the garden shed. Not to mention, spending endless hours cooped up at home gives me too much time to think.

I've always believed in everything in moderation, and thinking is no exception.

My mother always tells me, "Overthinking ruins relationships." I suppose she would know since she's been married and engaged more times than I can count. Codependence aside, there's no denying the woman gives solid advice. For someone with a hot-mess love life, she's astoundingly perceptive, so I'm taking her words to heart and trying not to think too much about Wells's protectiveness. His intensity is one of the first things that caught my eye the night we met. In my club-going days, I loved nothing more than a broken man in need of fixing, and Wells had broken-beyond-repair practically tattooed on his forehead.

There was a depth to him at a time when most men were terrified to dive below the surface.

He had a gaze that drank me in whole.

An enchanting half smile that felt like it was made solely for me.

He was sad and beautiful, intelligent and quiet.

As deep as the ocean.

We were as much alike as we were different—if that's even possible.

His charms are . . . different . . . these days.

"You're home early," I say when I find him hunched over the kitchen island, thumbing through his phone. "Thought you were staying late tonight?"

His coppery-green gaze flicks from his phone to me. The screen in his hand darkens with the touch of a button, and he flips it face down before sliding it aside and making me the sole recipient of his attention.

"Meeting got canceled." He makes his way to me, his hands lifting to cup my face before he collects his kiss. He tastes like spearmint with a hint of his afternoon cappuccino lingering on his tongue. His hands rove down my hips before he pulls me against him. "So I thought you and I could have a little . . . one-on-one meeting of our own . . ."

I place my palms against his shoulders and peel myself away with a chuckle.

"Going to pass on account of the porn-y pickup line. Think I deserve better than that," I tease. I didn't marry Wells for his way with words. Quite the opposite. The man can communicate with a look. A single curl of his lip. A straightening of his posture could command a room if the conditions were right. The man can disarm me with a single sideways glance or make me lose my train of thought the instant his fingertips graze my inner thigh.

Words, on the other hand?

Not exactly his forte.

His love language is *acts of service*.

I just never in a million years could've imagined his *acts of service* would one day feel like anything but.

He kisses me again, this time harder. Greedier.

"Babe, I'm sweaty." I turn my face to the side and his mouth presses against my cheek, his lips arching into a smile.

"Since when has that ever stopped me?" he tries to pull me into his arms again, but I back off.

Six months ago, we decided to try for a baby, and at first it gave our lovemaking a carnal edge that it didn't have before. But with months of trying and nothing to show for it, the excitement is fading faster than either one of us expected. Though I suspect it isn't the lack of a pregnancy putting a damper on our sex life, but the fact that I'm becoming a hostage to his suffocating love, to his obsession, to his inability to be alone.

Wells holds me by my wrist, his fingers wrapped carefully around my pulsing flesh. The glinting look in his eye makes me think of a hunter with his prey in its scope.

"Let me take a shower first, okay?" I fan my face and offer a humble smile, one that suggests I'm not playing this game tonight.

The glimmer in his expression a moment ago vanishes, and he releases my wrist from his grip. Disappointment colors his dark eyes, and I hate that I put it there. He's a good man. He has a good heart. And he loves the hell out of me. I don't know if I feel the same anymore—but it doesn't mean I want to hurt him.

"We'll pick up right where we left off." I lean in and kiss him on the cheek—a sweet peck to lift his spirits. I don't stay to watch the disenchantment spread from his eyes to the rest of his face. The number of times I've turned him down, I can count on one hand. But I need to wash the sweat from my hair and clear the dizzying thoughts from my mind . . . if that's possible.

Too many times, we've let an incident with my stalker ruin a perfectly good night.

I can only imagine that's the stalker's whole point . . . to scare me.

To wreck my mood.

To haunt my dreams.

To be that familiar and sudden chill down my spine when I'm in a crowded space.

Once upstairs, I toss my gym bag on the bed, peel out of my leggings and tank top, and step into the shower.

Fifteen minutes later, I'm toweling off, inhaling the steamy, lavender-scented air and feeling better equipped to wear a brave face as I attempt to enjoy this evening with my husband.

Wrapping my wet hair in a towel, I grab my robe off the hook and step into our bedroom—only there's a dark figure seated at the edge of our bed.

A blood-curdling scream escapes my lips. I'm frantically covering my body with the sheer fabric of my crepe robe when I realize it's only Wells.

"Relax, relax . . . shh . . ." His soothing voice fills the space between us, and when he rises I instantly recognize his shape.

"You scared me." I lightly pound at Wells's chest when he gathers me in his arms. "My heart's beating so hard right now."

The sun had been setting when I'd first stepped into the shower, and I hadn't thought of turning on a lamp so I wouldn't be stepping into a pitch-black room. I used to take my spin classes in the mornings, but ever since the stalker's activity ramped up this month, Wells has instructed me to mix it up, to get out of anything remotely resembling a routine. He's even gone so far as to rent me a new car every week so that I'm harder to follow, harder to find.

Still, whoever they are had no problem finding me today.

"You're tense," he says as his hands knead into the small of my back. "Everything okay?"

My lips part, ready to tell him about the letter on my windshield tonight, half tempted to steal the desire from his eyes and send him into another obsessive spiral.

I don't want to be a prisoner in this house anymore.

Or a prisoner of his love.

For now, I let my robe fall, until it pools at my feet, and then I press my mouth against his. I like us better when our bodies do the talking, when words aren't getting in the way of everything else. I learned long ago that sex is just sex. It's emotions that complicate things.

A busy body quiets the mind.

"You just scared me, that's all," I say between kisses that now taste like his favorite gin. "Sitting there in the dark like that."

"Who else did you think it would be?" he asks as he tastes his way down the side of my neck.

I only wish I knew.

15

SYLVIE

I'm striding down the upstairs hallway the next morning when I hear Wells's voice trailing from below.

"This is the third time this month," he says, tension spiking his tone.

I stop in my tracks, ears perked. Wells isn't normally one to lose his temper.

"I think I've been more than generous with you over the years," he says next. After a long pause, he adds, "I'm aware that's how you feel. You've made yourself clear a number of times, but my stance hasn't changed. I won't be making another deposit this month."

Exhaling, I continue on.

He must be on the phone with Mary Claire.

When Viviette passed years ago, she left 90 percent of her estate—Westhaven included—to Wells. Everything else went to various staffers and charities. Ever since then, Wells and his birth mother have been attempting to patch their tattered relationship, realizing that all they had left for family was each other. Somewhere along the line he purchased her a two-bedroom bungalow in Santa Monica as well as a Mercedes-Benz.

In addition to that, he gives her a monthly stipend, though he's never shared exactly how much she receives. Given his generous nature,

I can only imagine it's a lavish amount. He says it's a drop in the bucket for him, that it isn't about the money as much as it's about being the bigger person. He said he couldn't live with himself if he pocketed all of Viviette's money and let the woman who gave him life become destitute.

After Viviette's passing, Wells claims he was just as shocked as Mary Claire was when Viviette's attorney read her will to them after the funeral. Viviette and Mary Claire's relationship had always been tumultuous, but writing her out completely was a cruel way to cap a lifetime of difficult and unresolved emotions.

I wish I could say I feel for Mary Claire, but after seeing the way she treats my husband, I can safely say there isn't an ounce of compassion in my heart for the miserable, entitled woman.

I find him seated at the kitchen table, and I wait until he ends his call before making my presence known.

"Morning," I say, sliding my hands around his shoulders from behind and depositing a quick peck on his cheek. Heading to the coffee maker, I pour myself a cup before joining him again. "Everything okay?"

Breathing out, he sinks back, staring out the window ahead, beyond the pool where the empty guesthouse sits. At one point, Mary Claire asked if she could sell the bungalow, pocket the funds to start some new business venture, and live there. When Wells told her no, that's when all hell broke loose, and she's been making life difficult for him ever since.

A few months ago, I suggested he go radio silent on her in the name of setting healthy boundaries. And he did. Until she had a health scare that landed her in the hospital for a week.

To this day, I'm convinced she manufactured each and every ailment, making some cocktail of symptoms into a mystery diagnosis requiring a myriad of tests and sympathy visits. It's impressive the way she plays him like a fiddle, excavating and exploiting his weaknesses. Getting inside his head. Textbook narcissists tend to have emotional manipulation down to a science.

"Mary Claire has her hand out," he says. "Again."

I pretend I didn't hear the end of his conversation a moment ago.

"I told her no," he says. "Obviously."

I sip my coffee. "Her persistence is impressive. It's too bad she doesn't do something more productive with it."

Early in our marriage, I learned to be careful in criticizing Mary Claire. As much as she makes Wells's life a living hell sometimes, he's oddly protective of her. While both of us are adopted—though our circumstances are quite different since I was adopted out of the foster care system as a teenager and he was signed over to his grandmother as an infant—there's no denying the undercurrent of abandonment that always seems to be there in the background.

"What's your schedule for the day?" he asks. I wish I could say he was simply making conversation, but I know the real motivation behind his question. He wants to keep tabs on me . . . for "safety" reasons.

"Thought I'd do some laps in the pool and then head into the office around ten." I take a drink of coffee. After last night's stalker scare, I'm not feeling like going to the gym today. I'll burn off my excess energy here at home. "I should be home by dinnertime."

Reaching, he places his hand over mine. His skin is ice cold, but the way he looks at me washes me in pure warmth.

Without a word, he rises, kisses the top of my head, places his coffee mug in the dishwasher, and grabs his briefcase and a roll of blueprints off the counter.

"I'll see you tonight," he says, keys jangling in his hand.

My phone chimes almost the instant he's gone.

TOM—You going to be around later today?

My stomach somersaults as I read the text from my ex, and while every fiber of my body is screaming at me to ignore, to delete, to ignore his efforts like I promised myself I would a million times before—my fingers are already busy tapping out a response.

Sometimes I think it wouldn't be the worst thing if something terrible happens to me, if the stalker one day takes things too far.

I'm an awful person.

God knows, I'd deserve it.

16

SYLVIE

"Sometimes I think marriage is a trap." My neighbor Portia is complaining about her husband again, which is all she ever does anymore. With an eighteen-year-old son almost ready to fly the nest, I don't understand what's keeping her here. If she's truly this miserable, she should leave. "No, I take that back. I don't think it is. I *know* it is."

"Life is short and there's no reason to spend a minute of it in a soul-sucking marriage," I say, leaving out the fact that I've been doling out that same advice to myself lately.

"You and Wells make it look so easy," she says. "What I wouldn't give for an ounce of what you two have."

"Looks can be deceiving. No marriage is perfect."

"Trouble in paradise?" she asks with a raised eyebrow. "I'm sorry. Don't answer that. It's none of my business. It just makes me feel better knowing that beautiful people have problems, too."

She chuckles, placing her hand on my shoulder like she's making a joke. But they say all jokes are rooted in truth.

The back door to the kitchen opens and slams, and a second later, Olly tromps in. He kicks off his sneakers, tosses his Nike backpack on the floor, and raids the fridge.

"Hi, Olly," I say with a smile in my voice. Portia has mentioned before that he has a difficult time socializing and there's no doubt he's a hard shell to crack, but I've been chipping away at his ironclad facade since the moment we met.

Not to compare him to an abandoned shelter dog, but I pride myself on breaking down walls: human or otherwise.

"Hi, Mrs. Westmore," he says, though he keeps his back to me. We're making progress. That's all that matters. It wasn't long ago he wouldn't even make eye contact with me.

He turns around, a stick of string cheese in one hand and a bottle of orange juice in the other.

"How was school?" Portia asks.

"School was school." He shrugs, fidgeting with the flimsy plastic wrapper on the cheese until she swoops in and saves the day. I've never been a mother and it's not my place to judge, but I can't help noticing how much she coddles him. "Thanks."

He turns, disappearing into his room a second later.

"Lee wants a baby," Portia says, keeping her voice low. "And I'm not exactly a Fertile Myrtle right now. That window's not only about to close, it's about to be nailed shut. I mean . . . if he wants one the old-fashioned way. And even then . . ."

"Do *you* want a baby?"

"I want security," she says, ever the candid woman. "I'd rather be miserable and not have to worry about money or a roof over my head or a car payment than be happy and living hand to mouth. Maybe it's messed up, but it's how I look at it."

"It's understandable given your previous circumstances."

I'd hate to be the baby used as a pawn in all of that, but it's not my circus or my monkeys nor is it my place to critique someone else's life decisions. I have no doubt people do this sort of thing every day, all over the world. There are fewer life bargaining chips more powerful than a brand-new human life.

Babies change everything.

Sometimes for better, sometimes for worse.

"I feel like I've been in survival mode my whole life, like I've been holding my breath for decades," she says. "I don't know any other way to be. Maybe one of these days I'll finally exhale."

Portia moved to LA when her son was an infant, waiting tables to pay for rent and formula. She had nothing and no one. And then somewhere along the line she met Lee—a cocksure entertainment lawyer who spared no expense molding her into the quintessential SoCal housewife. She told me all of this the very first time we met on the sidewalk between our homes. I was going for a run and she happened to be outside deadheading the endless rows of red peonies that surround her picture-perfect house.

"What about you? Do you and Wells want a family?" she asks.

It's an invasive little inquiry given the fact that our budding friendship has yet to so much as blossom. We've hung out a handful of times lately, and only another handful of times with our husbands in tow—two men who couldn't be more different from one another.

"Maybe someday," I say, hoping she lets it go. Just this morning, Wells reminded me to make an appointment with some hotshot fertility specialist in downtown LA. Now that we have six months of fruitless efforts and I'm in my midthirties, his impatience is starting to show.

The other day I told him that maybe we weren't meant to be parents. The crestfallen look on his face told me everything I needed to know about his feelings on the matter.

But the idea of carrying Wells's child, of being tied to him that way for the rest of my days, has recently lost its luster.

I can't have a baby with a man I'm thinking of leaving. It wouldn't be right. And it certainly wouldn't be fair to the child.

My phone vibrates in my hand, and I check the screen to see Wells's name flashing across it. He's probably wondering where I am, why it took so long to run out and grab the mail.

"Sorry, I need to take this." I wave my phone. "See you around, okay?"

I leave with a smile that hopefully disguises the dread coursing through me, and I amble back to Westhaven, each step heavier than the one before it.

"On my way," I say when I answer his call, skipping the formality of a simple "hello." Never mind that I forgot to grab the mail. Portia flagged me down before I had a chance. I make a quick detour to the mailbox by the gate.

"That's not why I was calling," he says.

"O-okay. What's going on?" I grab an armful of our mail—the newest issue of *Architectural Digest*, a thick pamphlet of fast food flyers and mattress store ads, and a small assortment of bills.

"I think you should come home right away," he says.

"Wells, you're scaring me," I say. "Did something happen? Is Mary Claire okay? Are *you* okay?"

"Just . . . come inside." He exhales into the receiver, and my stomach sinks.

Whatever this is—and it could be a number of things—it isn't good.

17

SYLVIE

"You can't tell me this isn't you." Wells all but shoves his cell phone at me.

A photo fills the screen. Zoomed in. Crystal clear.

A woman entering a hotel in the afternoon.

There's no denying it's me—black yoga pants, white tank top tied just above the waistband, hair tucked under a coffee-colored baseball cap that practically blends in with my hair.

"Who sent you this?" I ask.

"Who do you think?"

"I don't know," I say, handing the phone back and tossing my hands up. I'm not sure whether to be creeped out that someone took my photo without my knowledge—or upset that my emotional affair has finally caught up to me.

This is what I wanted, though, right?

In a way, in the deepest planes of my existence, a part of me wanted to get caught so Wells would finally see that he deserves better than me . . . so Wells would finally let me go.

"Care to tell me what you were doing at the Beverly Hills Richmond Hotel yesterday at one o'clock in the afternoon?" His jaw is tight, clenched, and his stare is sharp, narrow, slicing through me.

I could tell him the truth—that I met up with my ex and had every intention of burning our marriage to the ground via self-sabotage. Then I chickened out. I couldn't go through with it. But with this photo of me going to a hotel in the middle of the day when I was supposed to be at my office, how could I expect him to believe anything I say?

"Who sent you that?" I ask again.

"Does it matter?" His forehead is all lines and he takes an incredulous tone with me. I don't know how to answer that. I suppose it doesn't matter—the damage is done. The cat is out of the bag. The truth always comes out and here it is, staring us in our faces. "Why, Sylvie?"

"Does it matter?" I echo his question.

Wells slams his balled fist on the counter, sending a start to my heart. I take a step back, inserting some distance between us.

"God damn it," he says before dragging his palm across his mouth. It takes a second for me to realize his anger is self-directed. "Sylvie, I'm sorry."

I'm the one who should be apologizing, not him.

His reaction is normal. Healthy. Understandable.

The man has just been betrayed by the woman he loves.

"Who is he?" Wells asks. "Wait. I don't want to know. I don't want to know anything. What you did or didn't do . . . none of it matters. Just . . . tell me how to fix this."

A hundred times I've played this scenario in my head and not once did it go this way.

"You want to *fix* this?" I ask, speaking carefully.

He closes the gap between us, gathering my hands in his. "I know I've been working a lot lately, and I haven't been as attentive as I should be. I don't want to lose you, Sylvie. I can't lose you. You're my everything. You know that, right? I . . . this . . ."

Wells's words fade into nothing, but his dark gaze holds me prisoner. A blanket of ice-cold trepidation runs through me.

I don't want to know the thoughts behind those eyes.

The man proposed six times before I finally said I'd marry him; if only he'd have taken "no" for an answer the first five then we wouldn't be here, both of us hurting for reasons of our own. One of us wanting out, the other desperate to hold on to a marriage that clearly isn't working.

"End it, Sylvie," he says before heading upstairs. He stops after a few steps. "Or I will."

18

SYLVIE

"So that's when I told your brother I was absolutely not going to invest in his start-up," my mother waxes on over the phone. "He has no idea what goes into a proper business plan. Up until a year ago, he was still wanting me to make his doctor's appointments for him. I told him to finish his business degree at USC and then we'll talk opportunities. Between you and me, he's not exactly a self-starter, so ideally we could find a business that's already up and running that he can just buy out . . ."

I let her ramble, as she tends to do during our weekly phone calls, and I work in a handful of "yeahs" and "mm-hmms" whenever she takes a breath.

"I think it's great he wants to be his own boss," I say when I finally get a chance to talk. As the youngest in the family, Monte has always struggled with doing things for himself and staying motivated. "Maybe this could be good for him?"

"But an ice cream shop?" She laughs, like Monte's idea is cute and comical. "Out of *everything*. It's not like we don't already have enough of them . . . I swear a new one crops up every other week around here."

"If it's what he wants to do . . ."

"Mrs. Westmore, sorry to interrupt." Our housekeeper, Kathryn, peeks her head inside my bedroom door. "You have a visitor."

"Who is it?" I mouth as my mother continues to talk.

"Mary Claire," she says. "She's at the gate. Should I let her in?"

Within seconds, a text from Mary Claire fills my screen, followed by a call beeping in.

She's not going to be ignored.

"Mom, I'm going to have to call you back," I say.

My mother doesn't ask if everything's okay, nor does she seem bothered by the sudden end to our conversation. I'm convinced that sometimes she calls just because she has no one else to talk to and wants to hear the sound of her own voice—which I've always thought was part of the reason she adopted three teenagers from foster care. With her husband working seventy-hour weeks and all of her extended family on the East Coast, she was lonely, needed someone to talk to, and didn't want to have to change diapers. That's where we came in.

Of course, it's more complicated than that.

Everything always is.

And she's not a bad person, per se.

She just . . . is who she is.

Ending the call, I instruct Kathryn to let Mary Claire in, and then I head to the closet to change out of my loungewear and into my work clothes since I'm heading to my office in the next hour. If I'm dressed like I'm headed out the door, maybe she'll keep her visit short.

I can't imagine what she could possibly want—though based on her recent conversation with Wells, I suspect it's money.

"Mary Claire, hi." I force a cordial smile when I find her in the living room a few moments later. She's leaning against the fireplace mantel, examining a photo of Wells and me from a Hollywood Bowl concert two summers ago.

She places it back and dusts her hands, as if holding the thing disgusts her. I don't even think she realizes she's doing it, but I couldn't miss it if I tried—just like I can't miss the half smile on her scarlet lips that comes off as more of a half sneer.

"Sylvie," she says, straightening her shoulders. "I was in the area and hoped we could have a little chat."

"About?"

"About Wells . . . who else?" She sniffs.

I make a show of checking my watch. "I'm supposed to be at the office in a half hour."

"This won't take long," she says with an impressive amount of confidence. "So I'll cut to the chase . . . you need to leave Wells."

"Excuse me?" If I leave my husband, it'll be on my terms, not because Mary Claire wants me to do it.

"I know about your"—her eyes slowly drip the length of me—"extracurricular activities."

"My what?" I play dumb. Any conversation with Mary Claire tends to be a game of chess, not checkers.

"I know all about that man you visited at that hotel. Your ex-boyfriend . . . Tom Briggs."

My lips part but nothing comes out except air.

She wasn't bluffing.

"Oh, don't act so surprised. Did you really think you'd get away with it?" she asks.

I remain silent. There's power in silence.

A different boyfriend I had a lifetime ago who was a skilled negotiator in the business sector always told me, *"When in doubt, say nothing. The one who speaks first, loses."*

"Who do you think sent Wells the photo?" she continues with a proud glimmer in her eyes. "It cost a pretty penny having you tailed, Sylvie. Fortunately Wells footed that bill—even if he didn't know it."

"Why would you do that?"

"Because I had a feeling about you," she says. "A feeling I haven't been able to ignore since the moment we first met. I wanted to confirm my suspicions. Peace of mind is priceless."

"How long have you been following me?"

She toys with the diamond pendant dangling from her suntanned décolletage. "Oh, sweetheart, no. *I* wasn't following you. I paid someone to do that for me. I have better things to do with my time. Did I not make that clear?"

"Were you having me stalked, too?" I ask.

Mary Claire wrinkles her nose, taking a step back. "What? No. Never. That isn't my style."

As much as I don't want to believe her, I do. If she admitted to having me followed, why wouldn't she admit to that, too? They're both equally heinous.

"You hurt him by sending that photo, you know," I say. My original plan was to leave him and pray he didn't find out about the almost-affair. Not because I wanted to cover my transgressions, but because I didn't want to add to his pain.

He may be intense and overbearing at times, but he means well.

And he's loyal to a fault.

He deserves better than me, even if he refuses to see that just yet.

"No, Sylvie. *You* hurt him," she counters. "Which is why you're going to leave him so he can find someone more suited for his needs."

"That's not up to you."

"He only wanted you because he couldn't have you. You know that, right? And now that he knows you're seeking affection in the arms of another man, it only makes him want you more. That's how this works."

"What does that have to do with anything?"

"He doesn't love you. He only thinks he does because he places you on this pedestal where you certainly don't belong. You're a club girl. An opportunist."

"You don't know a damn thing about me."

"I know more than you think I do." She shrugs, her lanky shoulders lifting to her blonde bob. "Anyway, you're clearly unhappy in this marriage. And we both know he deserves someone who appreciates him. Why don't you just leave so you can finally put everyone out of their misery?"

Blood runs hot through my veins, creeping up the back of my neck and stopping at my tensed jaw.

"Leave," I say through clenched teeth. Pointing toward the door, I add, "Now. You're no longer welcome in our home."

She lingers in place, maybe to piss me off, maybe because she's too stunned to react just yet. I've never kicked her out of my house or spoken to her like the scum that she is.

After an endless moment, she turns on her heel and shows herself out.

With my heart hammering in my teeth and adrenaline rattling through my bones, I take a deep breath, collect myself, and head to the office.

Her words play on a loop in my head all afternoon.

She isn't wrong.

19

SYLVIE

I make my way to Portia's the instant I get home from work. With Lee always working and Olly spending time with friends, she's always happy to entertain my company. I'm still rattled from Mary Claire's visit earlier, still trying to wrap my head around her audacity. When Wells gets home in an hour or two, I'll fill him in. I tried calling him earlier, but he was in meetings all day, and I didn't want to burden him with family drama.

Until then, I'll bide my time with Portia, who has become an unlikely friend.

My only friend these days, really.

At times I feel awful for not inviting her over to the house. She's hinted a few times about wanting the "official tour of Westhaven," but I know if I open the door once, it'll become a regular thing, and these days, going to Sylvie's has become a respite from my everyday life.

Portia's a breath of fresh air compared to the people I ran around with in my twenties and early thirties—all of whom have distanced themselves from me since my marriage. Judging by their very active social media accounts, they're still the kings and queens of the nightlife scene, still burning the midnight oil in the trendiest clubs and bars.

In the early days of our relationship, I used to be able to convince Wells to go out with me once a month, and we'd always meet up with my old friends. But after a few times, it was clear Wells wasn't enjoying himself. Not only that, I was becoming more out of the loop with their goings-on than ever, which relegated our conversation to awkward small talk.

I was officially the boring married friend—the afterthought of the group.

"Hey, stranger," Portia says when she answers the door. "What's going on?"

"Just wanted to stop by and say hi," I lie. Sort of. I want to say hi, but I also want a distraction from everything. And a drink. Portia makes the best drinks. I kind of want to vent, too. My head is so filled with bottled-up thoughts that it's pounding. It can't be good to keep everything in to the point it causes physical pain.

"Come on in," she says. "You can hang out while I make dinner."

I follow her inside, immediately met with the mingling scents of her signature gardenia-coconut candles and a savory suppertime dish.

"You're welcome to stay and eat with us," she says. "I'm making beef and barley stew—Olly's request. Never mind that it's, like, a hundred degrees outside. I've never understood the appeal of eating stew on a hot day. It's like drinking iced coffee in the winter." She shudders. "Can't do it."

"Thank you, but I'll pass on the soup." I take a seat at her kitchen island.

"Good call." She tosses an ivory kitchen cloth over her shoulder and measures a handful of spices before dumping them into the stockpot on the stove. "Can I get you something to drink?"

"I thought you'd never ask."

Turning on her heel, she tosses me a wink. "I know you, baby."

Heading to the beverage fridge under the counter, she grabs a bottle of chilled vodka and a can of organic pineapple juice. Last time she told me she buys those just for me. I wasn't sure whether to be appreciative or to take that as a sign that she can't pass a carton of pineapple juice without thinking of my drink of choice.

"There you are." She slides my drink across the marble island, stopping for a moment to take me in. "You doing okay?"

In all the years I spent running around with my former friend group, no one ever took the time to memorize my favorite drink or ask if I was okay. Portia may be my only friend at the moment, but she also may be the only real friend I've ever had.

"It's been a day," I say with a sigh.

"Tell me about it." She covers my hand with hers. "I mean, literally. Tell me about it. What happened?"

Wells is huge on privacy, and I've never been one to air my personal dirty laundry, but I don't know that I can keep this in any longer.

"Wells's biological mother stopped by today," I say. "She, uh . . . asked me to divorce him."

Portia's jaw falls. Snapping a hair tie from her wrist, she ties her hair back into a messy top knot and takes the barstool beside me.

"Oh, my God," she says. "Who does that? And why?"

Half of me wants to tell her everything.

The other half of me knows there's no coming back from that once I do.

Her image of me will forever be altered.

As much as I try not to care what people think of me, there's a small part of me that loves how much Portia adores me. It makes me feel like maybe I'm not all bad. I want, so badly, to be the person Portia thinks I am and not the confused, wavering woman I see in the mirror every day.

"She's never liked me," I say, opting not to get into the nitty-gritty just yet.

"Okay, but there are mothers-in-law all over the world who can't stand their son's wife—most of them don't show up at your door demanding you get a divorce. Something had to have triggered this—unless she's just batshit crazy. And in that case . . . all you can do is ignore her."

"Ignoring her tends to only make things worse," I say. "It works for a little while, and then she comes back full force with some new kind of drama or ailment or conundrum. It's uncanny."

I'd have never been able to tell my old friends this sort of intel. It'd be spread all over town by the next day and halfway to New York by the weekend. That group loved a good, old-fashioned fall from grace.

While I don't miss them, per se, I miss the excitement they brought to my life.

Never in a million years did I think a marriage could be this lonely.

"What did you tell her?" Portia asks.

"I told her to leave. And then I went to the office. After that, I came straight here. I couldn't even bring myself to go inside my house when I got home today. It was still too fresh, too tainted."

"What did Wells say about it?"

"Wells wasn't there, and I haven't told him yet," I say. "He was in meetings all afternoon."

"I'm sure he'll deal with it," she says. "In-law stuff can be so touchy sometimes."

I have no doubt that Wells would deal with it if I asked him to, but do I want him to? Is it worth it? What's the point when I already have one foot out the door anyway? It seems like it'd be wasted energy.

"The crazy thing is . . ." My voice shakes, and I stare down at my pineapple vodka, watching the ice melt in real time. "If I tell you something, Portia, I need you to promise, to swear, you won't repeat it to anyone. Ever."

Her eyes widen and she nods. Dragging her fingers across her chest, she makes the shape of an X.

"Promise," she says. "I won't tell a soul."

"I've been thinking, for a while, about leaving Wells." The words feel hollow coming out of my mouth, as if someone else is saying them and not me. For a brief moment, I'm certain I've exited my body.

She's studies me.

"I thought you two were happy?" she finally says a moment later. "What's going on?"

"I just don't think marriage is for me."

"All of a sudden? How long have you two been married now?"

"Three years," I say. Three suffocating years. "I thought it was what I wanted. Now I'm not so sure."

She rests her head on her hand, still staring at me, hardly blinking. Almost like she's in shock. And maybe she is. She thought we were the "perfect" couple. This must be blindsiding her.

I twist the oval diamond ring on my left ring finger, which dazzles in her soft kitchen light. It was a vintage heirloom piece that once belonged to Viviette—a token of one of her many failed engagements.

Maybe it's cursed.

I sniff a laugh, quietly chastising myself for redirecting the blame to an inanimate object.

"He's not the same person he was when we got married," I say, "and neither am I."

"No one ever stays the same."

"True. It's one thing to evolve as a couple. It's something else entirely to change so much you bring out the worst in one another."

"Have you thought about marriage counseling?"

I shake my head. "He has no idea I'm feeling this way."

She exhales, pinching the bridge of her nose. "There's got to be a way to fix this."

"I don't know that I want to fix it." Burying my head in my hands, I add, "I feel like a caged animal, Portia. I'm isolated. I'm suffocated. And at some point, I think I fell out of love with him. Once you fall out, it's hard to fall back in, you know?"

Her lips press into a hard line.

"My mind is pretty much made up," I continue, "but God, I hate to give Mary Claire the satisfaction. That's what kills me the most. Okay, I take that back. Hurting Wells is what kills me the most. But giving Mary Claire exactly what she wants? That's a close second."

"Screw Mary Claire and what she wants. Whatever decision you make, it's for yourself. If she wants to take credit for it, then let her. It won't affect you one way or the other. Once you leave—*if* you leave—she'll be dead to you, right?"

"I guess." I sip my watered-down drink, giving it a swirl first.

"How do you think he's going to handle this?"

"Not well."

And that's putting it lightly.

"He'll be heartbroken," I say. "Devastated."

We sit in mutual silence for a beat or two, lost in our own thoughts.

"I almost slept with someone else," I add. I might as well get it all off of my chest.

Portia gasps. "For the record, I'm not judging you . . . I'm just shocked. Never pegged you as anything but loyal to Wells."

"It was an ex and it would've meant nothing, and I changed my mind before we even made it to the hotel room." I lift a flattened palm. "Not that it makes the whole thing any better. I just . . . I wanted to feel something again."

Dirty. Worthless. Alive. Free.

Everything all at once.

I don't pretend to understand it.

"They say infidelity affects 50 percent of marriages," Portia says. "It's more common than you probably think, so don't beat yourself up."

The timer on her stove chimes, and she abandons her perch beside me to tend to her stew.

A strange chime plays across both of our phones at the same time, sending a startle to my heart.

"It's just the National Weather Service," she says. "Like we didn't already know we were in a heat wave . . ."

"Ugh. Rolling blackouts expected tonight," I say.

"Of course." She taps her wooden spoon on the side of her stockpot before grabbing her phone. I assume she's texting Lee. Or Olly. A minute later, she gathers candles from a nearby cupboard, as well as a power bank and two flashlights. Next, she places her phone on its charger. "Oh, geez. I just texted Olly to tell him to get home, and apparently he *is* home. Says he's been home all afternoon. Mother of the year right here. Can't keep track of my kid."

"In your defense, he's pretty quiet."

"Right? Like sometimes I want to tell him to blare some music or something. Be a regular teenager. He's a good kid, though. I could have it way worse."

I toss back the remainder of my cocktail with a hard swallow and rise from my seat.

"I should probably head home and wait for Wells," I say, not even disguising the unease in my voice. I'm not looking forward to telling him about Mary Claire's visit . . . nor am I looking forward to pretending everything is fine for one more night. But if we're already dealing with an impending blackout, there's no need to add more fuel to an already stressful fire.

I'll tell him tomorrow.

I'll tell him he needs more than I can give him.

More love, more respect, more loyalty, more *everything*.

Tonight, I'll be a caged animal.

This time tomorrow, I'll be a free bird.

20

SYLVIE

"I wasn't sure where you kept the candles," I say when Wells gets home. I'm rifling through the kitchen cupboards in search of a flashlight, a taper candle, a box of matches—anything. "The east half of the county is already blacked out. Lost all power. Everything."

"I heard." He shrugs out of his navy suit jacket and hangs it on the back of a kitchen chair before unfastening his watch and setting it aside. I'm not sure if I'm imagining it, but his movements are slower today. More calculated. Careful. As if he's biding his time before spilling what's on his mind.

"So . . . do you know where a girl can find a candle around here?" I ask, half teasing in a pathetic attempt to keep things light to make up for the tension in the room.

Without answering me, he heads to his bar cart, fixes himself a gin and tonic, and then disappears into a hallway. A minute later, he returns with an old hatbox filled with flashlights, candles, and matches. I didn't know that box existed until now.

"Mary Claire stopped by today." I slip my hands into my back pockets. Clearing my throat, I add, "Things got a little heated."

He sips his drink, peering at me over the rim of his crystal tumbler. "I know."

"You know?"

"She told me."

"Before or after?" I ask.

"After," he says. "I never would've allowed her to come here if I knew what she was going to say to you."

His unwavering loyalty is vindicating and heartbreaking at the same time.

Again, I don't deserve him.

"Did she also tell you she's the one who sent you that photo?" I ask. We haven't spoken about the almost-affair since he told me to end it. Either he's still processing it, or he wants to sweep it under the rug and move forward. "She was paying someone to tail me . . . with the money you were sending her."

He takes another drink. "Not surprising."

"I was pretty shaken up after she left," I say.

"I'll bet." His phrasing is sympathetic but his delivery is not.

Wells has always been a man of few words, but tonight his words are fewer and farther between than ever. With every tick of the grandfather clock in the hall, the tautness in the room ratchets up a notch.

He takes a seat at the table, drink in hand, and stares out the window, toward the dark, empty guesthouse.

"You're extra quiet tonight," I say.

"Don't have much to say right now."

I know Wells enough to know that when he's quiet, it's because his mind is busy.

"I don't think you should hang out with Portia anymore," he says.

"Wait, what?" I almost choke on my words. "Why?"

"I don't think she's a good influence on you."

Releasing an incredulous laugh, I say, "In case you forgot, I'm a grown woman and no one influences me."

"You've changed," he says, glancing sideways at me. "Since you've been hanging around her more. You're not the same."

I place a hand on my hip and march toward him. "And you don't think that maybe, just maybe it all coincides with the stalker incidents and you locking me down like a prisoner in my own home? Curfews? Extra cameras? Passcodes? Telling me when I can and can't go to the gym or what route to take to work? You don't think my changing has anything to do with your obsessive need to control my every move?"

Wells slams his drink onto the table. Clear liquid sloshes over his hand, spilling onto the polished walnut tabletop. He ignores it.

"For the record, she's a phenomenal friend," I say. "Probably the best friend I've ever had, and that's saying a lot because I used to think you were my best friend. Now I know you're just a man who can't stomach the idea of being alone."

"Excuse me?"

"I almost slept with another man, and all you did was slam your fist on the table and tell me to end it," I say. "And for the record, there was nothing to end. We had lunch. He wanted more, but I refused."

"What did you want me to say? To do?"

"I don't know—maybe put me in my place? Tell me how much I hurt you? Show an ounce of authentic emotion?"

He winces. "*That's* what you want?"

"You don't love me for me, Wells. Let's be honest for a second. You love my company. You love not being alone. But you don't love me. If you did, you wouldn't have swept that whole thing under the rug like it was nothing."

"So now you're telling me how I'm supposed to feel?"

"No," I say before changing my mind. "Yes, actually. I am."

"Doesn't work that way."

"When you love someone and they betray you, you should feel something. Anything."

"Just because I have a different way of showing my emotions, doesn't mean I feel nothing."

"Fine." I cross my arms. He isn't entirely wrong. But still—his reaction wasn't fitting. In fact, it wasn't much of a reaction at all.

The kitchen lights flicker. Within seconds, the space we share goes pitch black save for the soft glow of the twilight sky outside the window. Without the hum of the fridge, we've got nothing more than the dark silence to keep us company.

It won't be long before the house becomes sticky and stifling in this heat with no power to circulate and cool the air inside. The idea of sleeping in a hot bed next to Wells after the day I've had holds zero appeal, so I head for the stairs to pack a bag.

"Where are you going?" he calls.

"To Bakersfield. I'm staying with my brother tonight," I say. It's a good two hours north of here, notably cooler, and there are no massive power outages. Getting out of town might take ninety minutes itself with all the traffic and nonfunctioning stoplights, but I'll sit in a car for hours if it means not spending the night in this oven-hot jail cell.

A minute later, I'm seated on the floor of my closet, tossing clothes into an open suitcase when Wells's dark silhouette fills the doorway. I draw in a startled breath. He's always so quiet, which makes it feel like he's sneaking up on me. While it's likely due to the plush carpet and the tiled stairs that don't squeak the way wooden ones would, it's unsettling just the same.

"Packing an awful lot for someone spending one night away." He slides one hand into the pocket of his slacks while the other one is gripped around a freshly topped-off gin and tonic.

"I'm just grabbing random things," I say. And it's the truth. I'm not thinking about tomorrow or the day after that.

His dark eyes skim the mountain of clothing before returning to me. He takes a slow sip of his drink, calm and collected.

A chill runs through me.

Rising, I zip my suitcase as fast as I can without making it obvious that he's worrying me, and then I wheel it to the hallway.

He follows.

Naturally.

But I ignore him.

Stopping in the kitchen, I grab my keys and toss them in my bag before heading for the back door next as it's the closest exit. I can't leave here soon enough.

One step outside and I'm engulfed in sauna-like heat, making my clothes cling to my body in an instant. The heart-shaped pendant on my neck—a gift from Wells's mother years ago—sticks to my flesh. I've always loved the classic, timeless look of it, and despite my differences with Mary Claire, it's something I've worn with pride. I should have left it behind, seeing as how I won't be a Westmore for much longer, but it's too late now.

The pool is still and glass-like without the pump running, and the darkening sky is filled with stars. It's a stark and peaceful contrast to the events of the day, but I don't stick around to enjoy it.

Dipping my hand into my bag, I feel around for my phone so I can let my brother know I'm on my way. Only the familiar pebbled leather case is nowhere to be found. In my haste to leave, I must have forgotten it on the charger in the kitchen.

I abandon my heavy suitcase by the pool and turn to head back to the house—only before I take a single step, an arm reaches around my neck, placing me in a choke hold. With my windpipe blocked, I'm unable to make a sound. Another arm circles my waist, pulling me tight against them.

Digging my fingers into my attacker's flesh, I claw and scratch and kick as I fight for air. But it's no use—it only makes them squeeze me harder.

My vision fades in and out as I struggle for oxygen, but I refuse to give up. I'm not going down like this, not when I'm twenty feet from my car, from freedom.

Ramming my hips back, I knock my attacker off balance, but their hold on me remains tighter than ever.

The serene view around me diminishes to a murky blue-gray as my sight grows dim.

And then . . . when I least expect it . . . I'm thrown like a rag doll into the pool, hitting my head on the way.

In a flicker of a second, I catch a glimpse of my attacker.

Everything goes black after that.

PART III
PRESENT DAY

21
JADE

"Not going into the office this morning?" I ask Wells when he kisses me at the breakfast table. He's been home less than twenty-four hours, wasted no time making up for lost time last night, and now he's cozying up to me in his favorite monogrammed robe and house slippers, settling in with a cup of coffee and a dimpled smile he wears only for me.

Before, when I'd look at him, I'd be instantly awash with warmth, a feeling I could only describe as *home*.

Now, there's this staticky feeling running through my middle.

It isn't good, but it isn't bad.

A cocktail of trepidation and denial?

"Thought I'd spend the day with you," he says, his strong hands cupping a pitch-black porcelain mug. "Haven't seen you all week. That and I'm absolutely spent from this trip. Need a day or two to wind down and recover."

Wells is a routine guy. An introvert. Too many things going on at once combined with too many people sucking the lifeblood out of him zaps his energy and makes him retreat into his shell. I don't relate, but I understand.

"What's your schedule like for the day?" he asks.

"Actually, Mary Claire invited me out for brunch," I say. She texted me last night, shortly after seven, with a last-minute invitation to some new reservations-only place on the beach in Santa Monica.

He lifts a brow. "Really?"

"Why do you act surprised? We kind of hit it off this week . . ."

He shakes his head, like he's shaking off his thoughts and replacing them with new ones.

"It's just not like her to be so . . . amiable," he says.

"People change all the time."

"That they do." He takes another sip, letting his attention veer toward the pool area outside. From this angle, I can't tell if he's simply looking out the window or if he's focusing on the guesthouse.

I'd give a million pennies for his thoughts.

"I'm not leaving for another two hours," I say. "Was going to try to write a couple of chapters before I left, but I can scrap that plan and we can do something if you'd like?"

He nods, lips pressed into a disappointed half smile.

"I'm sorry—I didn't realize you were going to stay home today," I add. "I can cancel brunch? I'm sure she'll understand."

"No, no. Don't cancel or change anything."

"Do you want me to ask if you can join us?" I can't imagine she'd say no to her son accompanying us.

"Wouldn't dream of crashing your girl time," he says with a wink. "I'm actually thrilled that she's making this kind of an effort with you. It's not her style."

"She told me I was a keeper—after we met at the coffee shop earlier this week. For whatever reason, she likes me I guess."

He rolls his eyes. "Everyone likes you, Jade. You're impossible not to like."

"Tell that to my college roommate." I take a drink of my tea and silently tell myself it's time to get up and start writing. But my mind is filled with questions for Wells and my body is anchored to the chair.

After a bout of quietude, I say, "Mary Claire isn't shy about sharing her feelings about Sylvie."

He sits his mug down, jaw flexing like it's a sore subject for him.

I didn't mean to strike a nerve.

"Those two were oil and water," he says. "There were a lot of heated exchanges over the years. The whole thing was disappointing to say the least."

Is he pointing fingers at Mary Claire? Sylvie? Or both?

So far, Mary Claire doesn't seem like one to mince words. But from what I know about Sylvie, she wasn't exactly a shy wallflower. I have no doubt she was able to hold her own.

"I was thinking . . ." I change the subject, assuming his silence means he's not going to sit here and explore the topic with me. "With Sylvie finding out that you've moved on . . . maybe I could spend some time with her? In some roundabout way, maybe it would help?"

Wells clears his throat and repositions himself in his chair. "Not sure that's a good idea."

"Can we at least try? Maybe I can go over there a few times a week, read to her, talk to her, treat her like a human being and not an incapable toddler? I mean, have you ever heard the way some of the nurses talk to her? They treat her like she has the cognitive level of a toddler."

"Maybe she does."

With all of his money and resources, I find it difficult to believe no doctor's ever been able to diagnose her, but it's not my place to question that.

"She's not the most cooperative person," he adds. Angling toward me, he places his hand over mine. "Your heart's in the right place, Jade, and I know that, but I don't want you to get hurt. Sylvie can get violent sometimes. We're lucky she didn't burn the house down the other day. And God forbid, if she ever laid a hand on you . . . I'd never be able to live with myself."

"You think she's capable of those things?"

"She's unpredictable. You've experienced that firsthand."

"Still . . . can I at least try?" I plead with my eyes. "She can't be happy in there, all alone and isolated. She must be so confused, too. I want to help her. I want to talk to her, spend time with her."

His hand leaves mine and he retracts from me.

"Give me time to think about it," he finally answers. "I'll make some calls to her doctors and see what they say. I don't want to make anything worse for her than it already is."

While he has a point, I can't help but wonder . . . how much worse could it possibly get?

22

JADE

"You know, it's just so sad how much money he's wasting on that poor girl," Mary Claire stabs a bite of her raspberry crème brûlée french toast.

The ocean breeze glides through her blonde waves, and the bright blue sky and midmorning sun make her practically glow on this sixteenth-floor rooftop restaurant.

"He just keeps throwing cash hand over fist at all of these doctors and specialists and no one has been able to fix her," she continues. "He's in denial. She clearly has some kind of brain damage from her accident. It's sad, really, but she should be in a skilled nursing facility, around other people like herself—you know, so she has some company, activities, socialization, that sort of thing. I can't imagine spending the rest of my life in that tiny guesthouse. Could you? It can't be good for her."

I shake my head. "I think he's just doing what he thinks is best."

"I'm aware." She nods before chewing her food. Swallowing, she adds, "I just worry he's running through his inheritance like there's no tomorrow. By the time he wants to retire, there'll be nothing left."

Ah, so this is about money and not what's best for Sylvie . . .

"Facilities aren't cheap either," I say. "I think he feels better knowing he's supervising her care and he's just a few feet away if she needs anything."

"And has she needed anything since you've been there?" Mary Claire asks, chin tucked and voice low. "Other than the day she quote-unquote escaped?"

"I've only been here a couple of months," I say, pausing. "So far there was only that one day her nurse had a family emergency and had to leave."

She points her fork across the table. "See, that sort of thing would never happen at a skilled nursing facility."

I'd have to agree with her there, but I still think Wells is doing what he thinks is best, and no one else can make that decision for him.

I didn't come here with the intention of getting more "dirt" on Sylvie, but I'd casually mentioned that I was going to try to spend some one-on-one time with her and wondered if she knew what kinds of things Sylvie used to be interested in.

That's when the conversation got off track. Mary Claire told me Sylvie was only interested in things that sparkled, shined, or cost more than a month in a private bungalow at the Chateau Marmont.

"I don't think you need to worry about Wells's finances," I say. In the time I've known the man, I've never seen him buy a flashy watch or ogle a million-dollar sports car. He wears custom suits, but that's because in his line of work and with his level of clientele, he has to look like a top-tier professional. Wells isn't frugal, he's money conscious.

But the more I think about it, the more I wonder if it's because a significant portion of his money is going toward Sylvie's medical care?

"Do you know how much he's worth?" Mary Claire asks. "Did the two of you have that conversation before you got married?"

"I told him I didn't want to know."

She snickers, rolling her eyes. "Honorable but not smart."

A compliment *and* a dig—at the same time.

Something tells me it doesn't take much to land on Mary Claire's shit list.

"Did you sign a prenup?" she asks.

"Yes," I answer despite it being none of her business.

"And?" She lifts a single manicured brow. "Will you walk away with anything if this marriage goes south?"

I almost answer her before stopping myself. While Wells and I both agreed on signing a prenup, my biggest concern was protecting my intellectual property. Without a prenup, Wells would get half of any and all royalties from books written during the course of our marriage. Despite Wells's insistence that I receive a reasonable payout should our union last at least five years, the least of my concerns was ensuring I'd walk away rich. I just didn't want to walk away poorer.

"I'm sorry, Mary Claire, but this conversation is making me uncomfortable," I say, swallowing the hard notch in my throat.

My body tightens, as if I'm expecting some kind of dramatic reaction, but the lines around her eyes soften.

"Don't apologize, sweetheart," she says. "I'm the one who should be sorry. It's not my place to pry. I just don't want you to get blindsided if—God forbid—you two don't work out and you walk away with nothing because he spent it all on *her* . . ."

"I'll be fine either way." I fork a piece of scrambled egg, though my appetite has seemingly vanished over the past few minutes.

"I know I might seem a bit obsessed with this topic . . . I just wish you could've seen what it was like when they were married," she continues. "Sylvie shopped like it was her full-time job. Red-bottomed shoes. Limited-edition designer bags. Exclusive resort vacations. Red carpet charity galas. It was like she had this empty hole she was constantly trying to fill with beautiful *things* . . . and in the end, she still seemed hollow and miserable. There was no light in her eyes the last time I spoke with her."

I'm not sure why Mary Claire can't let this topic go. She's a dog with a bone, and I'm afraid to snatch it away for fear of getting bitten.

"My mother never should have disinherited me." Her eyes narrow and she places her fork down. "Now her life's work, her legacy, her fortune . . . it's running out. He's going to have to sell Westhaven one of these days. And he'll probably sell it to some new-moneyed jerk who'll raze the damn thing and put some kind of pseudo-Italianate monstrosity in its place."

"Sounds like what they did to Pickfair."

She straightens her spine. "Exactly. That's what I want to avoid. I still can't believe anyone allowed that to happen. Such a tragedy. I get so angry when I think about people destroying history like that. Pickfair was priceless."

"Wells is pretty protective of Westhaven. I doubt he'd sell it to someone who just wanted to tear it down. I think he'd rather subsist off ramen and peanut butter sandwiches than let go of his dream to turn the place into a museum."

She picks up her fork again. "I hope you're right."

Me too.

I hope I'm not wrong about anything related to Wells . . .

I've always been good at reading between the lines, especially where people are concerned. But still, I can't shake Portia's stories of his possessiveness. Alternately, was Portia exaggerating? I'm still getting to know her, and I don't quite have her pinned down yet.

"I, uh, heard through the grapevine that Wells was a little on the overprotective side with Sylvie," I say. "Do you think that has anything to do with him wanting to keep her close?"

Mary Claire almost chokes on her french toast.

Dabbing her mouth with her napkin, she places it back in her lap before leaning forward.

"You didn't know?" she asks.

"Know what?"

"Sylvie had a stalker," she says, leaning back. "I don't know that they ever caught the person or whatever came of that. The whole thing sort of . . . went away . . . after Sylvie's accident. I suppose when you never leave your house, the stalker has no way to follow you."

"I had no idea . . ."

"Oh, yes. Death threats and everything," she says. "It brought out a darker side of Wells. He tends to go to extremes where his loved ones are involved—if you haven't noticed."

"That's terrifying. I'm sure he was just trying to protect her," I say.

"Right." Gathering in a long slow breath, she turns her gaze toward the rolling ocean waves. "I'm sure that's all it was."

23

JADE

"When were you going to tell me Sylvie had a stalker?" I slip my purse off my shoulder and place it on the kitchen table when I get home from brunch.

Wells glances up from his laptop—so much for taking the day off.

Sliding his glasses down his nose, he places them aside before squinting my way.

"Mary Claire said Sylvie had death threats and everything." I take the seat beside him. "Is that true?"

His mouth forms a straight line and he clears his throat. "For a period of time, yes."

"And it's true you never figured out who it was?"

"Not for a lack of trying. I had every police department and three-letter agency in the area trying to track this person down. They stopped once she had her accident, and the case went cold."

"That must've been terrifying . . . for you and for her."

"To put it lightly." He leans back in his chair, arms crossed, a subtle sign that he's feeling the need to guard himself—or his emotions. "I don't like to think about that period of time if I can avoid it."

"I'm sorry—I hate to pry, but I was just shocked to find out about that. Do you think her stalker might have had something to do with her accident?"

He shrugs, arms still folded. "It's anyone's guess. We were in a blackout that night, no power. Security cameras were down. Exterior lights were off. Anything could've happened."

I swear his lower lip trembles for a moment and his hazel eyes turn glassy, but it all disappears in an instant and his expression returns to its stoic baseline.

"I hate to think that I didn't do enough to protect her." His voice is broken, but his face remains steely. "The ironic thing is . . . she was leaving me that night because I was *too* protective of her. I pushed her away when all I wanted to do was keep her safe."

I slide my chair closer to his and pry his hand out from under his other arm, taking it in mine. Saying nothing, I give him my full attention, silently letting him know I'm here for him.

"Looking back, I know I went to extremes," he says. "Hindsight being twenty-twenty and all of that. And I'm not proud of some of the things I did—even if I meant well. I treated her like a prisoner, and then I got angry when she told me she wasn't happy rather than sitting there and hearing her out."

"We all make mistakes."

"She was leaving to stay at her brother's the night of her accident," he says. "Said it was just for the night, but based on how much she packed, I knew she wasn't coming back."

My breath catches in my lungs. Is he confessing to hurting her?

"The fact that she was twenty feet away when that happened . . . in our own backyard . . . and I didn't hear or see a thing . . . it's something I still haven't been able to forgive myself for." He squeezes my hand, his eyes holding mine. "If I hadn't pushed her away, she wouldn't have been leaving that night, and none of this would've happened to her. She wouldn't be living in that guesthouse like a shell of a person."

"You can't blame yourself. You didn't hurt her."

"Not directly."

Rising, I throw my arms around his shoulders, breathe in his woodsy aftershave, and hold him tight.

"I won't make the same mistake with you," he says, his voice muffled against my neck. "Everything I did with her . . . I'm doing differently this time. I won't push you away, Jade. I won't let anything get the best of me ever again."

The pain in his voice runs straight through him and into me. Every fiber of my being knows he's a good man with a heart of gold.

I see it.

I feel it.

I *know* it.

My heart swells and breaks at the same time, and I kiss his lips as if to seal his confession, as if to tell him his feelings are safe with me.

"You okay?" I ask a moment later.

"Yeah." He gathers in a long breath. "Actually feels good to get all of that out."

"I wish you'd have told me sooner."

Wells cocks his head to the side. "Why would I want to burden you with any of that? Also, I'm not exactly proud of the way I acted. It's a period of my life I wish I could redo, not relive."

I can't blame him for not wanting to shout any of that from the rooftops.

We're all capable of doing things we're not proud of if the circumstances are right.

"I spoke to one of Sylvie's doctors today," he changes the subject. "Told him what you wanted to do. He said it would be worth a try, but he thinks I should be the one to explain your intentions. She needs to hear it from someone she knows and trusts."

My breath catches in my throat, but I contain my excitement.

"Of course," I say. "Whatever we have to do."

24

JADE

My stomach rumbles as we stand outside Sylvie's door. An hour ago, Wells and I were having dinner, but I was so anxious about visiting Sylvie that I could hardly take more than a few bites.

Wells raps on the door three times before letting himself in.

"Wait out here," he says. "It'll just be a couple of minutes."

The canvas tote bag on my arm holds a handful of books, a three-hundred-piece puzzle, a book of crosswords, and the latest issues of *Vogue*, *People*, and *Harper's Bazaar*. I wasn't sure what she was into, so I brought a little bit of everything we could use to pass the time with.

Two minutes later, Wells exits the house.

"I'm not sure what all she understands, obviously," he says, his forehead creased with worry lines, "but you're free to go in. I'll wait outside if you need anything."

I tilt my head. *"Wells . . ."*

"All right. Fine." He studies my face, though for what, I'm not sure. "Dr. Brunswick said we should start out small; ten or fifteen minutes and then build up from there."

"Got it."

Wells steps aside and I head in, shutting the door behind me.

Sitting in her recliner, a thick fleece blanket over her lap and staring dead-eyed at the flickering TV screen, is Sylvie.

Her nurse glances up from her spot in the kitchen, giving me a nod as if to confirm that she understands the plan.

I slip off my sandals and make my way to the sofa, sitting a few feet from Sylvie. Placing my bag at my feet, I pull out the things I've brought.

"I wasn't sure what all you were into, so I brought a little of everything." Retrieving the stack of books, I say, "We have *War and Peace*, in case you're into the classics. I also managed to get my hands on an advanced copy of Reese Witherspoon's latest book club pick . . . Then there's *The Life and Times of Serafina Dumont*—written by yours truly. If you're not a book person, we can do a puzzle."

I place the three-hundred-piece puzzle of a beachy sunset next to a lavender carton of Kleenex on her coffee table.

She tracks me with her eyes, but the rest of her body remains statue-still.

"I also brought some magazines." I offer her the *Vogue* issue first, but she doesn't accept it. I stack them next to the puzzle. "No worries. I'll just leave them all here."

Resting my elbows on my knees, hands clasped together, I offer her a smile.

"I know this must be weird for you," I say. "Probably safe to say neither one of us ever imagined ourselves in this position."

Sylvie's gaze rests in mine.

Leaning to the side, I glance into the kitchen where the nurse is on her phone, earbuds and all. We make eye contact and she smiles and nods, oblivious to what I'm about to say.

"I told Wells I wanted to spend time with you because I thought it might help you . . ." My words trail off. "After you, um, did what you did to my closet and bathroom . . ." I don't want to use words like ransacked or destroyed because that's not what this is about. ". . . It was clear to me that you're upset. I don't know if you're upset with Wells for moving on or with me for . . . I don't want to say taking your place because it isn't like that, but I think you know what I'm trying to say here. Anyway, I just want you to know that Wells loves you. So much. And I love him. So much. And all either of us wants is to make sure you're supported and have everything you need both physically and emotionally."

She blinks, returning her focus to the TV screen where some documentary on the golden age plays on the History Channel. The male narrator has a sleepy, monotone voice and the static images are mostly black and white. I find it hard to believe she's more interested in a documentary than this awkward-but-necessary exchange we're having.

"Are you a history buff?" I ask, switching gears in hopes of capturing her attention again. "I'm not sure if Wells told you, but I write biographies about powerful and notable women in history. I'm working on a book about Viviette right now, which is how I first met him."

Slowly, she turns her gaze to me.

I pull out the book I brought about Serafina Dumont and flip the cover to face her.

"This woman was an orphan in the 1920s. She was adopted by a wealthy family in New York. At fifteen, they married her off to a man three times her age—as part of a business deal between that man and her adopted father. She was treated terribly by her husband . . . back then women were still seen as property even in the upper echelons of society. Anyway, her story kicks off after the birth of her fourth child, where she almost died. It ignited something fierce in her, and she became an outspoken proponent of women's rights . . . it's fascinating stuff. I can read it to you if you'd like?"

She doesn't respond, not that I expected her to.

I steal a peek at the nurse once more, who despite being twenty feet away, might as well be on another planet. She's too focused on her phone, swiping the screen every few seconds, to be watching any of this.

Setting the book aside, I readjust my posture on her stiff sofa and prepare myself for the question that's been dancing on my tongue for days.

"Sylvie," I say, keeping my voice low. "I need to know why you keep telling me to run."

She looks down at her lap, her hands softly pulling at the fleece blanket.

"Are you telling me to run? Or are you asking me to help you run?" I clarify my question.

Her dull gaze returns to mine.

I scan the space we share for any scrap of paper or any random pen, only the place is clean as a whistle. Nothing but tissues, a half-empty water jug, a TV remote, and the items I brought.

Sliding my phone out from my pocket, I open my Notes app and flip it to face her.

"Can you type out a message for me?" I begin to hand the phone her way, only to stop cold when the nurse looks up from her phone. A cold sheet of panic flashes through me, and I pretend to accidentally drop my phone.

The nurse pulls her headphones from her ears, places her phone aside, and gets up from the table. Holding my breath, I wait for her to make her way to the living room to ask what's going on, only she turns once she reaches the hallway.

The bathroom door closes and locks a few seconds later.

We're running out of time. There's no guarantee when she's done in there, she'll go back to minding her own business with a screen in her face.

"I need to know what you're trying to tell me," I say, inching so close I'm nearly falling off the edge of the couch. She won't look at me now. "Sylvie, please."

I give her a moment before pushing again.

"Do you want out of here?" I ask. "Yes or no? Blink once for yes, twice for no."

Sylvie doesn't blink at all. I don't even know if she comprehends anything I'm asking.

"Do you want me to leave?" I ask in vain.

Once again, she doesn't blink.

I'm more confused now than ever before.

"Is anyone in danger here?" I ask. "Anyone at all?"

She turns to me slowly, only this time her eyes are brimming with tears . . . and she blinks once.

My heart sinks and my stomach unfolds.

"Oh, my God," I whisper. A hundred scenarios come to mind in an instant. "Did someone hurt you the night of your accident?"

Sylvie blinks.

"Did you see who did it?" I ask with my heart in my teeth and my pulse on fire.

She blinks once.

The bathroom lock pops from down the hall, and within seconds, the nurse appears, checking her watch.

"Mr. Westmore said he'd like the visit to be no more than ten minutes and it's been about fifteen," she says with an apologetic tone. "I'd let you stay a while longer, but we need to start Sylvie's night routine."

It's barely past seven o'clock . . .

"Of course." I collect my things in my bag and rise from the sofa. "Sylvie, I'll come by again soon, okay?"

She doesn't blink. She simply points her dead-eyed stare to the flickering television.

Does Wells know that Sylvie saw her attacker? That she's implying danger still lurks around here?

Trudging back to the main house with more questions than I had before, I find Wells in his study.

"How'd it go?" he asks.

I'm tempted to bring it up to him, but something stops me in my tracks. Wells told me she was trying to leave him the night of her "accident," and he's admitted to being overly possessive and protective. Portia and Mary Claire have corroborated this as well.

I scratch my mission—for now.

I need more time to dig because as much as I don't want to believe Wells was the one who hurt her, in this moment, it's the only thing that makes sense.

By keeping Sylvie here, is he trying to keep *her* safe?

Or is he simply trying to keep his secret safe from ever escaping Westhaven?

25

JADE

"Did you know Sylvie had a stalker?" I ask Portia the following morning. I should be tucked away behind my laptop, but ever since my time with Sylvie last night, I can't focus on work to save my life.

Portia places a handful of Cheerios on Lily's high chair tray and turns back to me.

"What?" Her eyes are wild. "No! This is news to me. Is that why he was always so protective of her, with the curfews and everything else? How'd you find this out?"

"Mary Claire mentioned it yesterday at brunch. I asked Wells about it afterward and he said she received death threats and law enforcement was investigating it and everything. Sounds like it was pretty serious."

She clucks her tongue and takes a seat next to me at the table while keeping an eye on her daughter.

"That's absolutely terrible," she says. "I wonder why she never told me about this?"

"Impossible to know now. People have their reasons for everything."

"Right, but she confided in me about wanting to leave Wells—why wouldn't she tell me about a stalker and death threats? Isn't that the kind of thing you tell your friends?"

I shrug and lift my hands. "No idea."

"Did Wells say anything else about it? Like do they think this person had something to do with what happened to Sylvie?"

"He said there's no way to know because of the blackout and the cameras being offline that night . . . but I can say he blames himself."

"For what? If he didn't do anything, why does he blame himself?"

"He thinks he pushed her away . . . I don't know. I just know it really weighs on him, and hearing everything he said puts it all into perspective—it makes this entire strange little living situation make perfect sense."

Lily shoves some Cheerios—as well as her sippy cup—off the edge of her tray. Portia wastes no time grabbing the items off her pristine floors.

"Did you know Mary Claire at all?" I ask. "When Wells and Sylvie were married? Or did Sylvie ever talk about her?"

"I met her a couple of times in passing. She was always kind to me." Portia slides her hands into her back pockets, glancing to the left like she's trying to recall what was said all those years ago. "But I also know at one point Mary Claire asked Sylvie to divorce Wells . . . the day before her accident, I believe? Somewhere around then. Everything sort of blurs together all these years later."

I should be surprised at Mary Claire's actions, but I'm not.

"Sounds fitting," I say. "Wait. Oh, my God." I clap a hand over my open mouth. "Do you think Mary Claire had something to do with Sylvie's accident?"

Portia frowns, her dark brows knitting. "Why would she want to stop her from leaving him? She wanted her to leave. If anything, she'd have been rolling out the red carpet and loading her luggage in the trunk of her car for her."

"Yeah, maybe . . . but yesterday at brunch, she seemed really preoccupied with how much money was left in the estate and how much Wells had spent on Sylvie during the marriage and since her accident . . . and she was trying to ask me about my prenup . . . is it possible she wanted Sylvie dead so she wouldn't be able to collect anything if they divorced?"

Portia angles her head. "Anything's possible."

A hush falls over the kitchen—until Lily interrupts it with a happy squeal.

"I think Sylvie saw her attacker," I say, biting the corner of my lip.

"Wait, I thought we didn't even know for sure if there was an attacker?"

"Right. But I visited her last night."

"You did?"

I nod, realizing I haven't shared the half of any of this Sylvie stuff with Portia. I've been guarding it like the mysterious enigma that it is.

"I asked her basic yes or no questions and asked her to blink once for yes and twice for no, and she implied she saw her attacker that night," I say.

"I thought she couldn't communicate," Portia says, "like, at all."

I shrug. "That's what I thought, too."

She squints before fussing with her hair, as if she needs some place to put her nervous energy. I used to think her enviable physique came from good genes or spending long hours on a Pilates reformer with a personal trainer, but now I'm realizing it's likely because the woman never sits still for more than a minute at a time.

"Jade, don't hate me for asking this, okay?" She winces. "But do you think there's any possibility—whatsoever—that Wells could've been the one who hurt her?"

Just a few days ago, she was the one swearing up, down, and sideways that Wells would never hurt Sylvie, that she was his "oxygen." Now she's singing a completely different tune.

Does she know more than she's letting on?

"Didn't we have this talk already?" I ask, injecting a lightness into my voice so as not to put her on the defensive.

"Yeah, yeah. We did." She waves her hand as if to write it off. "Sorry. I know I'm contradicting myself. I just . . . I want answers, like anyone else. It's not right what happened to her. It's not fair."

"We're on the same page there," I say before realizing I need to use the restroom. This morning with a head full of doubt, I went for a jog around the neighborhood, came back, showered, and chugged a liter of water before heading over here. "Do you have a restroom I could use?"

She points to the doorway in the back of the kitchen. "Of course. Olly's room is down the hall, you can use his bathroom. Second door on your right."

I make my way to Olly's hall bath. With a mountain of dirty clothes piled on the tile floor next to the shower and multiple dabs of blue toothpaste lining the sink, I'm shocked to see Portia lets him get away with this. For as much as she lives for her son, I've noticed she has a tendency to micromanage his every move and speak to and of him as if he's a kid and not a twenty-one-year-old grown man.

I'm finishing up a couple of minutes later, washing my hands, when I realize there's no hand towel hanging from the towel bar. There's a used gray bath sheet crumpled on the tile floor next to the toilet, but I'm not touching that with a ten-foot pole. I open the cabinet below the sink in search of spare washcloths or towels, anything clean that I can dry my dripping wet hands on, only something catches my eye . . . a glint of gold dangling off the side of a small ceramic jar.

Curiosity getting the better of me, I carefully slide the jar out and gently tug the gold chain.

My mouth runs dry and my face goes numb when I see what it is.

Resting between my fingers is a gold heart-shaped locket etched with the exact same ornate *W* as the locket Mary Claire gave me the day we met at the coffee shop.

She called it my "welcome gift," proclaiming that I was officially a Westmore now . . . she also mentioned she gave the same one to Sylvie.

If this one isn't Sylvie's . . . then it's one *hell* of a coincidence.

26

JADE

"Can I ask you something random?" I press my cheek against Wells's bare chest as we lie in bed, staring at a black void of a ceiling.

He sniffs, amused. "No such thing as a random question, but sure."

"Were Sylvie and Portia very close before the accident? How would you describe their friendship?"

Wells sits up slightly, his breath warm on the top of my head. "I take back what I said—that *is* random."

I've conjured up at least half a dozen scenarios to explain how Sylvie's locket made its way to Portia's son's bathroom only to deduce that the most logical, sane, and rational explanation is that she was there a few years ago visiting, used Olly's bathroom, the necklace fell off, and either Portia or a housekeeper or Olly tucked it away in the bathroom for safekeeping and forgot about it.

Every bone in my body wants to believe that's exactly what happened.

"Were they close?" I ask.

"They were spending quite a bit of time together right up until the accident . . . but it's the strangest thing; after Sylvie's accident, Portia never reached out, never came to visit. Didn't so much as send a card or flowers. I figured maybe she didn't want to impose. Some people get weird about that stuff, hospitals and sickness and near-death. I try not to assume, but I chalked it up to something along those lines."

I press my lips flat, remembering what Portia told me last week—that Wells wouldn't let anyone near Sylvie after her accident.

One of them is lying.

I opt to keep that to myself until I can do more digging, though Portia's son being in possession of Sylvie's necklace isn't working in her favor right now.

"Can I ask you another not-so-random question?" I cozy up against him, hoping my warmth will make him pliant and malleable and he'll continue to answer my queries without reading between the lines. "After spending time with her, I'm just trying to get the full picture here."

"Shoot."

"After Sylvie's accident, did her family ever come around?" In the two short months that I've lived here, working in a room with a direct view of the guesthouse, not once have I seen anyone go through that door besides Wells and her nurses.

He releases a long, slow breath. "Sylvie's mother passed a couple of months after the accident—glioblastoma. Five weeks after her diagnosis, she was gone. It happened so fast, we hardly had time to process it."

"Oh, my God. I'm so sorry to hear that. It must have been awful—for everyone."

"Sylvie wasn't able to attend the funeral, and I'm not exactly sure if she even comprehends that her mother is no longer with us . . . sometimes I wonder if that's a blessing in disguise. I can't imagine feeling grief and having no way to express it." He threads his fingers through mine before lifting the top of my hand to his lips. "Must be hell on earth."

"What about her brother? Is he around?"

"Which one? She has two. And no. Neither one is around. One lives in Atlanta, and I've actually never met him. The other lives in Bakersfield, and he's about as self-centered as they come. Once Sylvie was no longer his personal savings and loan, he wanted nothing to do with her. After I told him about the accident, he laughed and said, 'Serves the bitch right.'"

I shudder. "That's a horrible thing to say."

"If she didn't have someone to take care of her . . ." His voice tapers into nothingness, disappearing into the thin nighttime air. "I know it seems crazy, everything I do for her, but who else is going to do it, you know? I'm all she has."

My heart breaks for Sylvie; for the woman she was, the woman she is, and the woman she'll never have a chance to be.

I've written dozens of heartbreaking life stories in my budding career, but I've never watched one play out in real time, one that hits this close to home.

Wells yawns and settles into his pillow. I take that as a cue that this conversation is bookmarked for another time.

To be continued.

I wait for his breath to grow soft and steady before slipping out of his arms and reaching for my phone off the nightstand.

I can't possibly sleep with all of this information running wild through my head.

Tapping my photo icon, I pull up the image of the locket—one I snapped when I was in Olly's bathroom earlier because I wanted proof that I wasn't imagining it. My hands were shaking and damp and I was fighting just to breathe, but I managed to capture a picture before returning to the kitchen and offering Portia some casual excuse about getting back to work.

As far as I can tell, she thought nothing of it.

She even texted me a funny meme a few hours ago.

I darken my phone and place it face down on my nightstand. Staring wide eyed at the ceiling, I rack my brain for reasons why Olly would've wanted to hurt Sylvie. He would have been eighteen back then . . .

Were they sleeping together?

Was Olly fixated with her?

Was he her stalker?

And as with all things, anything is possible.

Lying in bed wide awake with all of these unanswered questions is doing me no favors. I toss the covers off and quietly slip out of bed and down the hall to Viviette's room. All of this energy needs to be funneled into something productive—for now.

I switch on one of the two starburst lamps and take a seat at her writing desk. Slipping on a pair of gloves, I select a journal from the stack and flip to a random page.

I'm afraid I've created a monster with Mary Claire, that I've spoiled her to a state beyond repair. What happened to girls being sugar, spice, and everything nice? Those sweet summer days with my tow-headed, happy little shadow are gone. Now she's blossoming into a young woman—and a frightful one at that. Pretty as a picture on the outside but her heart is darker than midnight. She's a brilliant, crafty girl. Terrifyingly, masterfully manipulative. I've watched her test her charms on the freckle-faced pool boy and college-aged gardener—costing both of them their jobs as I refuse to risk those types of liabilities.

My mother says Mary Claire is a typical teenager discovering puppy love for the first time. But I made her. I know her inside and out. My mother doesn't see what I see or feel what I feel. That sense of dread and unease when my daughter walks into the room. It takes a lot to rattle me, but there are times Mary Claire has me nervous with exhaustion . . . on the inside of course. I never let my true feelings show because God forbid she'll find a way to use them against me.

I've never met someone so adept at influencing someone else and making them believe it was their own idea.

I wish I could be proud of her. I wish I could say her headstrong determination is going to take her far in life. But something tells me those qualities will be the death of her . . . if they don't become the death of me first.

My daughter is nothing but trouble.

There's a circle-shaped dot near the end of the entry, where the paper was discolored by something decades ago. A tear, perhaps? A drop of brandy? Either way, Viviette was not in a good way when she wrote this. Even her handwriting is slanted, rushed.

I reread her entry again, sitting in stunned silence with the neatly scrolled words on the timeworn pages between my fingertips.

In all the diaries I've read so far, she has never spoken of Mary Claire in anything close to these terms. I check the date—June 17, 1973. Mary Claire would've been just fourteen years old, five years away from having Wells.

It's impossible to know if Viviette was simply being theatrical and dramatic—as was her nature—or if she was truly terrified of her fourteen-year-old. None of her other entries seem over the top or rife with embellished anecdotes.

Ice-cold chills trickle down my spine in the lamplit darkness of Viviette's bedroom. Perhaps it's all in my head, but I get the eerie sensation that I'm no longer alone.

Closing the diary, I snap off my gloves and head back to bed, crawling under the warm covers and curling up to my husband.

As questions pile on top of more questions, all I know is that I know nothing.

But tomorrow's a new day . . . and I won't stop until I find out exactly what happened to Sylvie that fateful night.

27

JADE

"Have you ever read Viviette's diaries before?" I ask Wells over breakfast the next morning. He's dressed for work in his signature navy blazer and suit pants accented by a crisp white dress shirt. He smells like leather and cash and looks like he walked off a studio lot.

I, on the other hand, just rolled out of bed less than five minutes ago after a less-than-rejuvenating night of sleep and definitely look the part.

"Absolutely not." He sips from his mug, his eyes wincing, though I'm not sure if it's because his drink is too hot or my question offends him. "It's an invasion of privacy."

"But not when I do it?"

"You're doing it for research purposes. It's different. Plus, if she ever had something on her mind, she had no problem sharing it with me."

"We still need to find the missing journals," I remind him.

"That we do."

"I couldn't sleep last night, so I tried to get some work done." I cup my palms around my warm teacup. "There was this entry she wrote about Mary Claire . . . said she was manipulative and terrifying."

Wells snorts a laugh. "Sounds about right."

"There was something she wrote that really stood out to me, though," I say. "She said Mary Claire could influence someone and make them think it was their idea—and mind you, she was referring to a fourteen-year-old girl at the time."

His chin juts forward as he contemplates this bit of information, and then he nods. "I believe it. She has the art of manipulation down to a science. That sort of thing doesn't evolve overnight."

"This might sound like it's coming from way out in left field . . . but do you think there's a chance Mary Claire had something to do with what happened to Sylvie?"

Wells almost chokes on his drink, catching a small amount of dribble with the back of his thumb before it stains his pristine white collar.

"I'm sorry," I say. "I didn't mean to catch you off guard like that, I just know the two of them didn't like each other, and Portia said Mary Claire had asked Sylvie to divorce you right before that happened . . ."

"Portia certainly likes to gossip, doesn't she?" He smiles, though his eyes are pained. "I can only imagine what she's told the neighborhood, but I try not to think about it. Anyway, yes. I've considered anyone and everyone who could've possibly had any reason to be near Sylvie that night, and I've ruled out Mary Claire. She was at home at the time—I know this because she asked me if I had a spare generator she could borrow since she was out of power, and then she wanted me to personally deliver it to her in gridlocked traffic. But no, it wasn't Mary Claire. The police investigated the incident inside out and upside down and they're adamant that Sylvie slipped and fell into the pool, hitting her head on the way. Broken pool tiles covered with her blood confirmed this."

He speaks as if he's rehearsed these lines before, as if he's had to explain himself six ways from Sunday to various inquiring minds over the years.

"At the end of the day, the facts remain unchanged. It was dark. The landscape lights were off. She had a suitcase and bag and she was in a hurry to leave. Evidence supports that she tripped and fell into the pool, hit her head, and sustained irreversible brain damage to her left hemisphere, thus affecting her speech and ability to communicate. If you'd like to take a look at her medical records, let me know and I'll dig them out."

"*Wells.*" I place my hand on his forearm and offer him a calm gaze. "I didn't mean to put you on the defense . . ."

His jaw flexes, though I don't take his frustrations to be aimed at me.

"Trust me, I'd love nothing more than to blame someone for what happened to Sylvie," he says. "It'd be a hell of a lot easier to stomach all of this if we had all the answers and someone to point a finger at. I'm doing the best I can with the information I have."

I squeeze his arm and offer him a reassuring smile. I feel awful he's starting his day so tense, so ripe with ancient emotions. But now that he's shot my Mary Claire theory down, I'm back to square one: Olly.

Wells checks his watch before swallowing the rest of his coffee and rising from the chair beside me.

"Before you go," I interrupt his mission. "I found something strange yesterday at Portia's."

"I don't think I've ever heard that woman's name this much in a twenty-four-hour period," he says, though I can't tell if he's teasing. "What'd you find?"

I tap my phone to wake the screen and pull up one of the images of the heart-shaped, monogrammed locket.

"What's this?" he squints, taking my phone and examining it closer.

"It's the same necklace Mary Claire has, the same one she gave me last week . . . when she said I was officially a Westmore. Sylvie had the same one, yes?"

He studies the photo for another moment before handing the phone back.

"She did. Never took it off either, which I always found odd since it was a gift from Mary Claire, but she loved that locket . . ." he says, his eyes still trained on my screen. "Where did you say you found that?"

"In Portia's son's bathroom."

Wells's naturally sun-kissed complexion turns a shade of paper white.

"The kid . . . what's his name again?" he asks.

"Oliver—Olly."

"Olly, yes. That's right." He begins to say something, then stops. "Damn it."

I nod, swallowing the impossibly large lump forming in my throat. "What are you not saying, Wells?"

He shakes his head, snapping out of it in an instant. "Nothing, I'm just . . . trying to make sense of it . . . but I can't. You said you found this yesterday?"

"Yep. I'd just washed my hands and I was looking for a towel, and I noticed this shiny gold thing sticking out of this—"

"Why didn't you tell me sooner?"

I realize we've only been together a year or so and there are still a million things he has yet to learn about me, but one of those—arguably the most important—is that I tend to keep my cards close to my chest.

"I wanted to sit with this for a minute, process it, make sense of it," I say. "That's why I was asking you all of those questions last night. And then when I saw that diary entry about Mary Claire being manipulative, I wondered if perhaps she orchestrated something using Olly—"

"Mary Claire has never met Portia or Olly . . . that I know of . . ."

"That *you* know of," I repeat his words slowly, carefully. "Portia said she met Mary Claire before . . ."

He stares straight ahead with his dark eyes unfocused and his hands gripping the back of his chair.

"I was thinking about casually bringing it up to Portia later today and—" I say before I'm cut off.

"*No.*" The boom in his voice startles me, and I jump back in my seat. "I'll handle it. You can't just go around accusing people of things. That and I don't want you getting involved."

"I wouldn't accuse anyone of anything, I'd simply ask her if—"

He slides his hand through the air, silencing me again.

"Please, Jade." He closes his eyes, swallowing. "Just . . . stick to finishing your book, okay? Let me deal with this."

"O . . . okay," I say.

He leaves me with a quick peck on the top of my head before swiping his keys off the counter and heading out.

I'm not sure how he plans to handle this, or how I could possibly write with this looming over my head all day, but I'm going to have to try.

There's nothing else I can do . . . for now.

28

JADE

"I think Portia's avoiding me," I say to Wells over the phone the next afternoon. "My last few texts to her have been left on read, and I've seen her out walking and driving by, so I know she's around."

"Wouldn't be the worst thing in the world," he says with a sniff.

"Did you say something to her about the locket?"

"Of course I did."

"When you said you were going to deal with it, I thought you meant you were going to have the police look into it. I didn't realize you were going to literally handle it yourself. What'd you say to her?"

"I asked her why Sylvie's necklace was in Olly's bathroom."

My cheeks flush red hot. If he'd have let me bring it up myself, I'd have been much smoother about it. I'd have found a natural place in the conversation to slip it in, and then I'd have gauged her reaction and gone from there.

These sorts of things require finesse.

Too late now.

"Wells . . ." I clamp my hand over my mouth, bracing for what comes next. "What'd she say?"

"That she was upset with you for snooping, and she didn't appreciate the accusation. Said for all she knew, Olly found it on the sidewalk, took it home, and forgot about it, which isn't completely out of the realm of possibility . . ."

"That was my first inclination, actually, but then you said Sylvie never took it off."

"Maybe the clasp wore out? No way to know for sure. Anyway, she was quite embarrassed and likely feeling a little betrayed since she thinks you were snooping through her son's bathroom."

"I was looking for a hand towel. Did you mention that?"

"Of course I did, but she was too upset to listen. She kept talking over me."

"I don't understand why you didn't just go to the police with this?" I ask.

"Sylvie's accident happened three years ago. Her necklace being inside a house she frequented doesn't exactly scream that Olly had something to do with any of this. The police would've laughed . . . I figured it'd be better to ask Portia myself."

"But what if he did have something to do with it?"

"It's a locket, Jade. Not a murder weapon."

"Then why did you get worked up when I told you about it?" I ask.

"I didn't get worked up . . ."

"You looked like you'd seen a ghost or that you were piecing things together in your head or something. I don't know. You looked . . . affected . . . by this information."

I hear his assistant in the background before he has a chance to respond, and I pick up a few of her words . . . *meeting . . . five minutes . . . Willis account.*

"I have to let you go," he says, his voice low in the receiver. "We'll finish this conversation tonight when I'm home." He pauses for an endless moment. "I love you."

I hesitate, too, though I'm not sure why.

"I love you, too," I say it back, though this time it feels different on my lips.

I know what I saw yesterday—I can still see his reaction plain as day in my mind's eye, the way the color left his face and his hands gripped the back of the chair so tight his knuckles flashed white.

Now he's acting as if *I'm* the one who made it into a bigger deal than it was.

Slipping into my tennis shoes, I grab my phone and keys and trek next door to fix this with Portia. I'm not sure if anything can be salvaged at this point, but I at least want to clear my name and let her know I wasn't "snooping."

Three minutes later, I'm standing on her front stoop, rapping on her door as I attempt to catch my breath. I was in such a hurry to get here, I practically sprinted.

The instant I hear footsteps on the other side of the door, my words are ready and waiting on the tip of my tongue—only when the door swings open, it's not Portia standing before me.

It's not Olly either.

It's a man with thinning salt-and-pepper hair, a heavy brow, and a thousand-yard stare.

I can only assume this is Lee—her philandering money-bags husband.

"Hi . . ." I muster up a friendly smile. "Is Portia around by chance?"

"And you are?" He asks the question like he already knows the answer, and his cold hard gaze drags the length of me and back.

I point next door. "I'm Jade."

"Ah, yes. The *new* Mrs. Westmore," he says with a sneer. "Well, *new* Mrs. Westmore, I'll have you know that Portia is beside herself, humiliated over all of this, and I'm not exactly pleased myself that she welcomed you into our home, only for you to go rifling through our son's personal effects."

"It wasn't like that at all."

He lifts a flattened palm. "I'll do the talking, thank you. Anyway, as I was saying, she's beside herself thanks to you. I hope you're happy with yourself, and kindly never darken our doorstep again."

With that, the door slams in my face.

29
JADE

"I'm officially blacklisted from Portia's," I tell Wells the instant he gets home that evening.

He shrugs out of his blazer and hangs it over a chair, as per usual.

"What are you talking about?" he asks.

"I went over to talk to her earlier, but her husband answered the door. Gave me an earful and then told me I'm no longer welcome there. I'm paraphrasing, of course, but that was the gist of it."

"You should have told me you were going over there." He slips his hands around my waist and pulls me closer, breathing me in.

"Why? So you could have stopped me?"

"Exactly." He steals a kiss—a sign that he's in a much better mood than the one I sent him out the door with yesterday morning.

Things were tense yesterday when he got home, but we kept our conversation neutral and by the time we went to bed, he seemed fine. This morning, he was out the door before I was up, which I worried meant he was upset with me all over again. But now here we are, like none of it ever happened.

"We can't go around accusing people of things," he says. "Especially when they're people we have to live next to. This whole thing is embarrassing for both of us now, and we all know Portia runs her mouth to anyone who'll listen. The rumor mill will be back up and running in no time."

"She's not going to say anything that would make her son look bad," I say.

"I'd hope not, but you never know with some people." He tips my chin up, stealing another kiss. "I just want to put this all behind us. Can we do that? Can we keep moving forward? Because I loved the track we were on until this little derailment."

I scrunch my nose at his words. "*Little derailment?* I was just trying to do what's best for Sylvie. Doesn't she deserve justice?"

"Justice for what? For falling into the pool and hitting her head? Not everything is some sensational story from one of your books, Jade." He lets go of me, pacing the kitchen. He grabs a fistful of his hair, but only for a second. "Sometimes terrible things happen to good people and that's that. Nothing's going to change what happened. And blaming innocent people years later . . . what good does that do for anyone?"

"How do you know Olly's innocent?"

"Innocent until proven guilty," he says.

"Don't you think we should at least have the police look into this?" I ask.

"I already told you, a picture of a necklace you found in the neighbor's bathroom isn't going to open an old case they solved years ago." Wells chuffs, hunched over the kitchen island. The tips of his ears are red and his cheeks flex with each taut breath. I've never seen him so worked up before. There's been more tension between us over the past twenty-four hours than there has been in the entire time we've known each other.

"I'm sorry if I made this complicated for you." I go to him, hugging him from behind, pressing my cheek against his curved back.

He turns around to face me, saying nothing.

"I just thought I was doing the right thing," I add, though my reason would make better sense with more context.

I still haven't told him about Sylvie's messages.

Run . . .

After the way he reacted to the locket—and then backtracked—I'm not sure I want to open up a whole new can of worms just yet.

"I'm going to go upstairs and give you some space," I say with the inflection of a tenderhearted preschool teacher. I've made a mess of his emotions lately, and the last thing I want to do is upset him any further.

I'm two steps away when he reaches for me, capturing my wrist in his hand and gently pulling me back to him, into his arms, holding me as soft as a delicate butterfly.

"Don't go." His plea is muffled against my hair. He exhales, his breath hot against my ear. "This whole thing is bringing out the worst in me, and I shouldn't take it out on you."

"I should've been more considerate of your feelings," I say. "I just thought maybe I'd found something significant, and I wanted to do the right thing."

Cradling my face in his hands, his eyes hold mine, and I'm washed in warmth for the first time in forever.

"I love that about you," he says. "But at some point, you have to stop taking on the problems of the world and focus on your own."

"I don't have any problems . . ." I'm half teasing, half attempting to prove a point. Everyone has problems. Mine just pale in comparison to his at the moment.

"Don't you have a deadline?"

"That's not a problem, that's just a deadline."

His mouth tips up on one side, the closest thing he's given me to a smile in days.

"I'm sending the chef home," he says. "And then I'm getting us a table at Pietro's. Think we could both use a change of scenery before we ruin a perfectly good evening."

30

JADE

I head to the checkout at the Suncoast Market—the little grocery shop a few miles from home. Armed with a birthday card for my mother, a bouquet of flowers for our housekeeper, Kathryn, because it's her twentieth anniversary of working at Westhaven, as well as a package of key lime tarts to share with Sylvie and her nurse when I visit later.

I'd meant to visit her last night, but Wells commandeered the evening with a last-minute dinner at Pietro's—a much-needed bright spot in the otherwise emotional week we'd been having.

Four people wait in line ahead of me. I steal a glance at the line to my right, counting a mere three people, only each of their carts are overflowing. To my left is another checkout with four people. Patience has never been my virtue, but I've got no choice but to wait this out like everyone else. It doesn't help that I'm anxious to see Sylvie again. After everything that has transpired the last several days, I'm praying I get a few minutes alone with her.

Balancing my shopping basket in one arm, I grab a nearby *Magnolia Home* magazine and page through it while I wait my turn. While some women might scoff at living in a home they can never remodel, I don't mind it. I'm a terrible decorator. I have no vision. But give me words, and I can piece them together perfectly in my sleep.

The line moves ahead, and I grab a different magazine—this time a gossip rag.

Some people wouldn't be caught dead reading one of these in public, but I've never been one to follow the crowd.

I'm engrossed in an article about Angelina Jolie and Brad Pitt's winery feud when something catches my eye. Glancing up, I spot a mop of inky-black hair and an imposing linebacker physique that can only belong to one person.

Olly.

My stomach drops.

I had no idea he worked here . . .

Or that he even worked.

Milk jugs and bread loaves look like children's toys in his generous hands as he places them carefully into brown paper bags and pushes them aside.

I let my stare linger in his direction for a few moments, hoping he notices, but he never looks up from his bagging job. Biding my time, I watch him work. He's careful, meticulous, quiet. While there's nothing wrong with bagging groceries for a living, I'm taken aback by the fact that Lee—with all of his connections—hasn't lined him up with an internship at some downtown law firm.

By the time it's my turn, my stomach is somersaulting.

"Paper bags okay, ma'am?" the teenage cashier with pink braces asks.

"Yes, please," I answer her, but I'm looking at Olly. Clearing my throat, I knock my knuckles against the conveyor belt to grab his attention. Then I smile. "Olly, hi."

He glances up, stops midbagging, then looks down again, returning to his work.

"Thirty-two dollars and eighty-nine cents," the cashier says. "Would you like to round up and make a donation to local homeless pets?"

"Sure," I say, still watching him. "I had no idea you worked here, Olly."

He ignores me.

"I really need to speak to your mom . . ." I say.

He places the last of my items in a brown bag and slides it my way. I take my bags, stopping for a moment when we're so close I can smell the abundance of men's body spray wafting from his person.

"Could you please have her call me?" I ask.

Without looking up, he says, "Why? So you can make up more lies about me?"

"It wasn't like that."

A vein in his forehead pulses, but the rest of him appears calm and collected.

"Why were you going through my things?" he asks, his voice low. "That's messed up."

"Why did you have the necklace?" I keep my voice down, too.

"You're going to get yourself in trouble," he says, visually scanning the space around us.

But before I can ask him to elaborate, a tall, thin man with a sparse mustache and gray tie wanders our way.

"Everything okay here?" he asks with a tone built for customer service. The badge pinned to his shirt says his name is Ron and he's the assistant manager.

"All good here." I smile and wave my hand. "We're neighbors . . . I was just saying hi."

"Olly, I need you bagging over on seven." Ron points to a checkout lane a few spots down where a cornucopia of scanned groceries are piling up.

While Olly heads to his new assignment, I return to my car.

Once home, I make my way to Sylvie's armed with key lime tarts and a list of questions I pray she'll somehow be able to answer.

31

JADE

"You're here just in time. I was about to change her bedsheets and tidy up a bit," Glenna answers Sylvie's door when I arrive. "Come on in, she's ready for you."

"I brought key lime tarts." I hold up the grocery bag. "Chef Margot said they're your favorite, Sylvie."

She's seated in her recliner in the living room, staring blankly ahead at the TV as she always does.

"Sylvie, did you hear that?" Glenna asks, ambling toward the recliner. She slides her arm under Sylvie's and helps her up. "Why don't I help you to the kitchen table so you can enjoy the treat Jade brought you."

"There's one for you, too," I tell Glenna.

She swats her hand. "Oh, you didn't have to do that. But thank you just the same. My grandmother used to make this every summer with limes from her lime trees . . . can't remember the last time I had one."

Glenna situates Sylvie at the table, and I take the chair across from her, setting out our desserts, napkins, and plastic forks.

"I'll be down the hall if you need anything," Glenna says.

Sylvie looks down at her tart, but doesn't reach for her fork.

The instant Glenna is out of earshot, I lean in. "Sylvie . . . we need to talk about the other day . . . when you implied that there was some kind of danger . . ."

Slow and steady, she lifts her gaze until it meets mine. Everything else about her is still and quiet.

"I have more questions for you," I say. "Can you blink again for me? Once for yes, twice for no?"

She blinks once.

My heart skips a beat, desperately hoping it wasn't a coincidence or a natural reflex.

"Before we begin . . ." I pause, not wanting to offend her but knowing I need to get this out of the way. "I was under the impression that you couldn't communicate. At all. Yet you've written me two messages and you're able to answer yes or no questions. Have you always been able to do this since your accident?"

She blinks twice.

I nod. "Okay. So this is something that just recently started coming back to you?"

She blinks once.

My stomach somersaults.

We're getting somewhere.

"Does Wells know you can do this?" I ask.

She pauses, then blinks twice.

"Has he tried to do this with you before?" I ask.

She blinks two times again.

The slam of the washing machine door echoes from down the hall. Glenna's likely almost done changing linens, so our time is limited.

"Last time I was here, you said you saw the person who attacked you," I say before squeezing my eyes tight. "Was it . . . was it someone you know?"

She blinks once.

My mouth runs dry.

"Was it . . ." I can't bring myself to say Wells's name, but I have to. "Was it Wells?"

She blinks twice.

I exhale and wordlessly thank God.

Tugging my locket out from under my shirt collar, I show her the heart-shaped pendant dangling from my neck.

"Mary Claire gave this to me last week," I say. "She said it was my *welcome to the family gift*. Did you have one like this?"

I unclasp it and hand it to her, it takes her a moment, but she finally accepts it, bringing it close for inspection.

A second later, she hands it back and blinks once.

"I found one just like this at Portia's house . . . in Olly's bathroom," I say.

Her eyes widen.

"Sylvie . . . did Olly hurt you? Was it Olly?" I ask.

The nurse returns, humming a catchy Rolling Stones tune before pouring herself a coffee from the carafe nearby. Grabbing an extra tart and a fork, she heads to the living room.

"Sylvie," I say, whispering this time. "Was it Olly?"

Her crystalline eyes brim with dampness, and a single tear slides down her cheek before she blinks a single time.

I clamp a hand over my mouth to muffle my gasp, not wanting to attract attention from the next room over.

Collecting myself, I follow up with another question, "Do you know why he would've done that?"

Sylvie blinks once, then after a quick moment, she blinks twice.

"Yes *and* no?" I ask. "Are you saying you . . . don't know for sure?"

She blinks once.

Glenna returns, grabbing the black nurses' binder from the counter as well as a pen. Stopping by the table, she chuckles. "Neither one of you have touched your dessert. Must be a pretty engrossing conversation you're having there."

If she only knew . . .

I slide Sylvie's tart closer to her and wait for the nurse to leave again.

"I want to help you, but you have to work with me," I tell her. "We have to be on the same team. You have to tell me everything, answer all of my questions."

Sylvie's gaze plummets to my wedding band before veering off to the side. Just like that, color leaves her face and any hint of light vacates her eyes.

Her body is still here, but her mind is light-years away.

In any scenario in which Olly is brought to justice—nothing will change for Sylvie. She'll still be here, a shell of her former self, divorced from the only man who loves her so much he orchestrates his entire life around her needs; a man who now seeks comfort in the arms of another woman.

The heaviness of this isn't lost on me.

And while Wells asked me not to get involved in any of this, how could I possibly walk away now? When we're so close to justice? To the truth?

"Sylvie, I need you to tell me with absolute certainty that Olly hurt you." Reaching across the table, I place my hand over hers.

She blinks. Once.

I collect my things, tell Sylvie I'll be back to see her again soon, and head straight to Portia's.

32

JADE

"What are you doing here?" Portia steps out onto her stoop, pulling her front door closed behind her. In all honesty, I didn't think she'd come to the door, let alone answer it.

"We need to talk," I say.

"Lily's about to wake up from her nap. And I don't have anything to say to you except leave me and my family alone." The liveliness that once resided in her spirit is gone, replaced by something darker, more ominous. "You're not who I thought you were."

"Portia, I'm not trying to hurt you or your family, and I wasn't snooping through Olly's bathroom the other day—I was looking for a hand towel."

"What's it even matter at this point? You found what you found, you made up some bullshit story, and your husband called and asked if my son, my *child*, hurt Sylvie. Do you have any idea how humiliating that is?"

I'd hardly refer to a twenty-one-year-old grown man as a child, but that's beside the point.

"I hear what you're saying, but you have to know something," I continue. "I've been spending time with Sylvie, and I've been able to ask her some questions, and it came out that she saw her attacker . . . and when I asked if it was Olly, she said yes."

Portia rolls her eyes. "Yeah, okay. Sure. The silent woman who hasn't said a word in three years is suddenly an open book, spilling all of her secrets now."

"Mock it all you want, but it's the truth," I say. "And when Wells gets home, I'll have her share it with him, too."

"Why are you here? Huh? Why are you telling me this? If you're so convinced my son did something, why didn't you go straight to the police?" She angles one hand on her hip.

"Because once I tell Wells about this, he'll go to the police. And all things considered, I still considered you a friend," I say. "I didn't want you to be blindsided when the police show up at your door."

"Oh, Jade. We're not friends." The condescending tone in her voice is as hurtful as the glare she's shooting my way. "Now Sylvie and I? *We* were friends. I've known you less than two weeks, and all you've done is manage to make my life a living hell. Friends don't do that to friends."

"I saw Olly this morning at the Suncoast Market," I say. "I asked him about the necklace and he said I'm going to get myself in trouble. Why would he say that?"

The menacing expression on her face fades. "He said that?"

I reply with an emphatic, *"Yes."*

Lowering herself to the concrete stoop, she takes a seat on the top step and rests her head in her hands. I take the spot beside her.

"God, he must be terrified," she says under her breath.

"So he did hurt her . . ."

Portia shakes her head. "He would never."

"Then why did he warn me?"

"I've never told you this, I guess because it hasn't come up in conversation yet, but Olly has a condition." Her voice trembles. "He's twenty-one, but cognitively, he's about twelve, maybe thirteen years old."

"Portia . . . I had no idea . . ."

"Because of this, he's always been easily influenced by his peers, and he doesn't always have the best impulse control," she continues. "It doesn't help that he's . . . different . . . from everyone else. He's quiet and he tends to get these fixations on things sometimes. He'll spend days in his room if I never make him come out. I thought having him get a part-time job at the grocery store would help get him out of this shell he's been in the past few years, but so far nothing's changed. If anything, he comes home from work and locks himself in his room every night. I'm lucky if I can get him to eat dinner half the time."

"You said it's been like this the past few years?" I ask.

"It's always been like this, but lately it's been worse than ever."

"Sylvie's accident was three years ago," I remind her. "Do you think . . . maybe those things are related?"

In my heart of hearts, I know they're related. I know what I saw in Olly's bathroom. I know what he said to me at the grocery store. I know what Sylvie's answer was when I asked her if Olly hurt her. I just need Portia to come to the conclusion on her own—for her own benefit. Her love for her son is the kind of mother's love all children should be so lucky to experience. I have no doubt she'd fight for him with her last breath, but what comes after this isn't going to be so easy.

"Sylvie was always so kind to him," she says. "Trying to pull him out of his shell . . . somewhere along the line, he took a liking to her . . . it was innocent . . . just a little crush . . ."

Her words fade, and she picks at her nails for a moment.

"Please, Jade." Portia turns to me, her eyes clouded with tears that spill down her cheeks. She doesn't swipe them away. "Olly would never hurt anyone. He's a good kid. He didn't do whatever you think he did, I promise you. I swear on my life."

I'm about to respond when the front door swings open and out walks Olly himself.

Portia quickly stamps out her tears on the backs of her hands. "Olly, what are you doing home? I thought you were working until four today?"

"Forgot to pack a lunch," he says, monotone. A black lunch bag rests in one of his hands, a bicycle helmet in the other.

"Where—where's your bike?" she asks, like a nonchalant mother asking a nonchalant question.

"Parked it on the side of the house," he answers her, though he looks at me. "I heard what you were talking about."

Portia waves her hand. "Olly, don't concern yourself with any of this, okay?"

"It's true," he says. "I hurt Sylvie."

Portia rushes up to her son, who makes her look tinier than she already is, and she lightly beats on his chest and tells him to stop talking.

"You don't know what you're saying, baby," she says. "It's okay, just go back to work and I'll see you tonight."

"Don't talk to me like I'm a kid," he says in a way that makes him sound like the very word he loathes. "I pushed Sylvie into the pool, Mom. I did it."

Portia covers her mouth, quiet, unmoving, as if she's letting reality sink into her one painfully silent second at a time.

"Who put you up to this, Oliver?" she finally speaks.

"I gotta go. Can't be late," he pushes past her, trots down the front steps, and disappears around the side of the house. A minute later, he emerges on his blue road bike, heading west toward the supermarket.

"Jade," she says when he's out of sight. "Please, don't do this to him. Please don't do this to me. To my family. He isn't able to fully understand the consequences of what he's done. I mean, you see what just happened. He's more concerned about going back to work on time . . . he doesn't understand the weight of what he just said, he doesn't understand what's going to come next for him. They'll stick him in some awful institution, and he doesn't belong there."

Her tearful plea shatters my heart in a million pieces.

"Then help me find out who put him up to this," I say.

She dries her tears once more on the backs of her hands.

"If someone truly put him up to this and he isn't mentally capable of understanding the consequences of his actions, they're not going to lock him up." I head to the front walk. "You have two days to get me a name—I can't keep this from Wells any longer than that."

Portia nods, slowly at first, then quicker.

She understands.

We're all on the same team here.

Team justice.

Team Sylvie.

Together we can give the silent woman the voice that was so wrongfully stolen from her three years ago.

33

JADE

My leg bounces as I wait for Mary Claire to arrive. After everything that went down with Portia and Olly yesterday, I spent the night making a list of anyone and everyone who may have benefited from harming Sylvie.

The stalker . . .
Portia . . .
Olly . . .
Sylvie's brother . . .
Wells . . .

Out of everyone, Mary Claire's list was hardly the longest, but it was the most compelling. From the moment we met, she made no bones about her distaste for Sylvie. The timing of asking Sylvie to leave Wells shortly before the accident happened also isn't helping her cause. Not to mention, her fixation with Wells's estate and her inquiry into our prenuptial agreement.

Any forensic psychologist will agree that money and greed are often driving factors behind murders, and while Sylvie wasn't murdered per se, it's safe to assume that the attack might have been an attempt gone wrong.

"There she is!" Mary Claire makes her grand entrance at the sleepy little seaside café I chose because it reminded me of the brunch spot she took me to the other week. I wanted her to feel comfortable and in her element so her guard is as low as possible. "My beautiful daughter-in-law. Look at you." She takes my hands in hers and opens my arms wide. "Radiant as ever."

Leaning in, she pecks the side of my cheek before placing her handbag in the empty chair between us and taking a seat.

Glancing around, she scans the room. "Where's our server? I'd kill for an ice water with lemon right now. I went hiking this morning with some girlfriends at Murphy Ranch and I must not have had enough water because I'm simply parched."

In the blink of an eye, she flags down someone else's server and gets her ice water with lemon, and manages to pull it off with charm and grace and not a shred of self-importance.

"I've never eaten here before," she says as she slides a pair of reading glasses over her nose. I can't help but notice the CC logo on the side. Chanel specs aren't cheap—especially when you're living on someone else's dime. "Love trying new places."

We place our lunch orders and make small talk while we wait, nibbling on french bread and seasoned olive oil while she tells me all about this nature hike group she found on Facebook. She reminds me of my own mother in some ways—always trying to make her life sound more adventurous than it is. Not that I can blame them. I don't suppose anyone wants to sound boring.

"Has Wells told you I've been spending some one-on-one time with Sylvie lately?" I change the subject when our meals arrive.

She peers over her glasses. "No, he hasn't. What kinds of things do the two of you do together?"

I get the sense she's asking out of morbid curiosity rather than genuine interest.

"So far nothing, really. I brought her some books and magazines and puzzles, but she hasn't seemed interested in any of those things,"

I say, biting my lip. I need to be delicate with what I share. This is chess, not checkers, especially if Mary Claire had something to do with Olly's actions. "You're not going to believe this, but I've gotten her to communicate a bit."

She ladles her soup but doesn't bring it to her rosy lips. "Communicate?"

"Yes and no questions. But yeah, we're conversing, I guess. In our own way."

"Interesting. And Wells is aware of this?"

Of course she defaults to Wells . . .

"Not yet," I say. "I wasn't sure how he'd handle it, given that she hasn't communicated with anyone in three years."

"Are you sure she's communicating? They're not tics or natural reflexes?"

"I'm positive," I say.

She sits straight, forcing a terse smile. "Well isn't that wonderful news? A modern-day miracle."

"It truly is. We're that much closer to finding out what really happened the night of her accident." I study her for a response . . . but her expression is poker-straight. Not a hint of worry or discernment anywhere. "In fact, she told me she saw her attacker, and she's already identified him."

"Him?" Mary Claire's brows rise. "I thought they ruled it an accident?"

"Guess they were wrong."

"So who was it?" she asks. "Who attacked her?"

"It wasn't Wells," I start out. "I had to get that out of the way."

Mary Claire exhales, stirring her soup. Is she relieved that it wasn't him? Or offended that I even asked? Either way, it doesn't matter. I'm on the precipice of truth here.

"Oh, before I forget," I say, wanting to get this out of the way in case our conversation sends her running. "I know it's a shot in the dark, but do you happen to have Sylvie's brother's phone number? The one in Bakersfield?"

I pull out my phone and prepare to add a new contact. On the off chance Mary Claire didn't put Olly up to hurting Sylvie, I want to rule out her brother who Wells claimed used Sylvie like his own personal savings and loan.

"Her brother in Bakersfield?" Mary Claire chuckles. "I think I met him once. At the wedding. Couldn't pick him out of a lineup if I tried. Now her mother, Cathleen, on the other hand, I think I might still have her number . . . assuming she hasn't changed it over the years . . ."

Mary Claire retrieves her phone from her bag.

"Wells said Cathleen passed away shortly after Sylvie's accident," I say with a flinch and a soft delivery. "Brain tumor."

Mary Claire stops scrolling through her contacts and peels her plum-colored Chanel glasses off her face.

"Wells told you that?" she asks, no inflection of any kind in her voice.

I nod.

"That's funny," she says. "Because I just saw Cathleen two weeks ago, at the Mar Vista farmer's market. Didn't talk to her because we were separated by a crowd of shoulder-to-shoulder people, but you can't miss that bright red hair anywhere. Or that distinct laugh of hers. Can hear it for miles."

"Wait, I'm confused . . . why would Wells lie about her mother being dead?"

Ignoring my question, Mary Claire wastes no time dialing Cathleen's number.

Everything is happening faster than I can process it.

"Cathleen, hi, it's Mary Claire," she says into the phone. "Going to put you on speaker if you don't mind. Anyway, just sitting here with a friend of mine." She shoots me a wink. "And we were talking about cats, and I told her about that cat you had that was the sweetest little thing. What breed was that again? The one with the round face?"

"British shorthair," a woman—presumably Cathleen—replies.

"Yes, British shorthair. That's right. I remember now. Could you text me the name of your breeder if you have it?"

"Of course," Cathleen says. "Just give me a minute or two to find it."

"Perfect. Thanks much, Cathleen. Take care." Mary Claire ends the call and places her phone down.

I'm unable to form a cohesive thought, let alone a sentence.

Mary Claire's ability to lie on the spot is nothing shy of impressive, but apparently so is Wells's.

What's that saying? The apple never falls far from the tree . . .

I grip the table as the room begins to spin, fading from light to dark and back.

The restaurant chatter around us diminishes into the background before everything turns black.

When I come to, I'm on the floor, surrounded by waitstaff, Mary Claire, and another patron who identifies herself as an ER nurse.

"Should I still call an ambulance?" someone asks, their voice sounding like it's coming from the other end of a tunnel.

"I think she'll be fine," Mary Claire says. "She just got a little lightheaded, didn't you, sweetheart?"

I attempt to sit up, only to be told by one of the faceless heroes around me to "take it easy."

"If you could box up our meals, that would be wonderful," Mary Claire says to one of the waitstaff. "And if someone could help me escort her to my car, that would be greatly appreciated. I'm going to get her home so she can rest."

"Ma'am, do you think you can stand?" someone asks me.

I nod. I'll sure as hell try.

On the count of three, they help me up. The floor beneath my feet is unsteady, slanted, but after a few deep breaths, everything around me straightens out.

"You don't have to take me home," I tell Mary Claire as she slips my purse over my shoulder.

Two waitstaff escort us to the parking lot, their arms linked in mine.

"Don't be ridiculous. You just fainted. You're not driving home and putting your life or anyone else's at risk." She points her key fob at her platinum Mercedes and presses the unlock button twice. The three of them help me into the passenger seat, and Mary Claire buckles me in. "There you are. I'll have you home before you know it."

She thanks the restaurant staff by tastefully slipping them some cash, and then she climbs in next to me.

"You really don't have to do this," I tell her as we back out of the parking lot, though I suspect it's too late. "I probably shouldn't leave my car here . . . it could get towed."

"Your car is the absolute least of your concerns right now," she says, her hands at a perfect ten and two on the steering wheel.

34

JADE

An Everly Brothers song plays softly from Mary Claire's speakers, and she taps her thumbs to the peppy beat, singing along under her breath with perfect pitch. Her ability to remain calm and take command of that situation is nothing short of remarkable, but not quite as remarkable as her ability to make up that cat story on the spot with Cathleen.

I'm not sure what's real or fake with her.

My phone vibrates in my bag, and I scramble to answer it, stopping when I see Wells's name on the caller ID.

"Telemarketer?" she asks when she senses my hesitation. "I've been getting a lot of those lately."

"No, actually, it's Wells." I wait until the call goes to voicemail before tucking my phone away. "I still can't believe he lied to me about Sylvie's mother. Who lies about someone being dead?"

"Wells," Mary Claire says without missing a beat. "Wells lies. Wells lies about everything, all of the time. The sooner you learn that, the better."

"It doesn't make sense . . ."

"It makes perfect sense if you understand how Wells operates." She steals a sympathetic glance my way. "And clearly, you're not there yet

". . . which is a good thing for you. Not such a good thing for Sylvie. Or Megan. Or Layla."

"Who are Megan and Layla?"

"Megan was the vet tech Wells dated before he married Sylvie—she supposedly moved back home to Tennessee, but I've searched her up I don't know how many times, and I've yet to find her. It's like she fell off the face of the earth. That or she ran away. Maybe she doesn't want to be found. Impossible to know. But before Megan, there was Layla—his college sweetheart. Poor Layla . . . she and Wells hit a rough patch shortly before graduation and she jumped off the Sixth Street bridge—back before they demolished it, of course."

"I'm sorry, but why should I believe anything you tell me? I watched the way you lied to Cathleen like it was nothing . . . I've heard all about how horribly you treated Sylvie . . . I've read about how manipulative you were to your mother . . . I don't know what your angle is, but—"

"—my angle?" She laughs. "You want to know my angle? Even if I told you, you wouldn't believe me."

"Try me."

We coast to a stop at a red light, and Mary Claire turns to me. "Believe it or not, Jade, but my angle is to save you."

"Save me?" I chuff. The last thing I've ever needed in my life is a savior. "From what?"

"From my son."

The traffic light blinks to green, and Mary Claire gently presses her foot on the gas pedal, her hands remaining at their prim and proper locations on the wheel, calm as ever.

"I'm taking you to Westhaven," she says, "I'm going to help you collect your things, and then I'm going to get you out of there before Wells gets home from work. It'll be . . . *easier* that way."

"What are you talking about? My husband lied to me—that's not grounds for a divorce."

Not yet, anyway.

I need to sort this out and make sense of it.

One thing at a time.

"Suit yourself." She sighs when someone cuts her off, but quickly regains her composure. "If you want to be just another Megan . . . just another Layla . . . just another Sylvie . . ."

"So you're saying Wells was responsible for everything that happened to all three of them?"

"That's exactly what I'm saying." She checks her side mirror and merges into a turn lane. From my calculations, we should be home in the next ten minutes, fifteen if we hit a bad pocket of traffic.

I think of Viviette's diary entry from the other night, about Mary Claire's terrifying ability to manipulate anyone with ease.

"Did you try to save Sylvie?" I ask.

"Of course I did," she says. "I tried my hardest."

"Then why were you so awful to her?"

"I saw how smitten she was with Wells, and I knew if I pulled her aside and told her what kind of person he truly was, she'd have laughed in my face and told me to get lost. So I thought I'd use a little reverse psychology. I was horrid to her. I was the mother-in-law from hell. I did nothing but cause issues in their marriage . . . anything from asking for money all the time to stopping by unannounced to flat-out demanding she leave Wells. I even went so far as to solicit an ex-boyfriend to try and woo her back into his arms—which almost worked until she couldn't go through with it." Mary Claire gathers a lungful of new-car-scented air and releases it, letting her shoulders fall. "Sylvie was a good person. She deserved better than him, and I hate what I had to put her through, but it was for her own good."

"Then why have you been so kind to me?" I ask.

"Thought I'd take the opposite approach with you . . . I figured if we could bond, have a pleasant relationship—or even a friendship—then I could at least be close enough to make sure you were safe at all times if, God forbid, something happened."

"How can you be so calm when you're talking about your son ruining all of these women's lives?"

"As opposed to panicking? What good would that do?"

She makes a right turn at the next light, putting us a few minutes from Westhaven.

"So if I grab my things, where am I supposed to go?" I ask.

"You're welcome to stay at my place in Santa Monica. I've got a pull-out sofa in the spare room. Or I can put you up in a hotel or short-term rental until you can get on your feet," she says. "Whichever you prefer."

"I can't afford more than a week in a hotel." And I don't want to think about having to pay back my advance. There's no way Wells will approve Viviette's biography if what Mary Claire is saying is the truth.

She swats her hand as if she's shooing a fly. "I'd be honored to help you get on your feet. I would've helped Sylvie, too, if I'd have had the chance."

"I don't understand . . . Wells said you didn't have any money, that you were constantly asking him for loans and handouts?"

"Like I said, that was just to put a little pressure on their marriage. I never needed a single dime from him. I've always been quite comfortable on my own, actually," she says. "But then I had to keep it up or else it would've been a huge red flag. Wells is smart, but I'm smarter."

"What about the stalker?" I ask.

"Wells," she says without pause. "No question. I have the photos to prove it, too. When I was having Sylvie tailed for that affair I was attempting to orchestrate, the private investigator I hired caught pictures of Wells leaving notes on her windshield a couple of times. I'm guessing he had some kind of tracking device on her car or phone. He always knew exactly where she was."

Mary Claire turns onto our street, and my stomach sinks with each passing house.

"Looking back, it was so obvious . . . he married this wild party girl believing he could tame her, and in the end, he had to convince her she was being stalked in order to keep her home, and as the stalker's notes became more aggressive, he kept her under lock and key as much as possible."

"She was leaving him the night of her accident . . . did you know that?"

She lifts her hand to her heart, her mouth curving down at the corners. "No. I didn't know that. How'd you hear that?"

"The neighbor told me. Supposedly she was good friends with Sylvie."

"I'm shocked she was allowed to have a friend . . ."

My phone vibrates again, only this time when I check the caller ID, it's Portia.

"Hey," I answer. "What's going on?"

"Oh, my God, Jade . . . oh my God . . . I had no idea . . . I . . . I didn't know . . ." Her words are parsed and breathless. "I had no . . . if I'd have known . . . I just . . ."

"What? What is it? What are you saying?" I ask.

Mary Claire shoots me a look.

"It was Wells," she says. "Wells put Olly up to it."

My blood turns to ice, but my skin is molten.

"How do you know for sure?" I ask.

"I know my son. I know when he's lying and when he's telling the truth," she says, "and he showed me the burner phone Wells gave him, the text messages, the Venmo deposits . . . they had this code word and this agreement that if Wells texted him the word, he would come over and . . ." She stops to catch her breath. "He would come over and scare her, assault her, whatever he had to do to make her feel unsafe, like she couldn't leave. He told Olly it was for her own protection, because she was safer at home than anywhere else. And of course Olly trusted and believed him. He paid him ten thousand dollars, Jade. Ten thousand dollars and now a woman's life is ruined—and Olly's life . . . I can't . . . I can't breathe . . . why would he bring my baby into this? My innocent son who would never hurt anyone?"

The pain in her voice is carnal, so full of torment I feel it in my bones just from listening to her.

"Portia, listen to me," I say. "We need to get Sylvie out of there immediately."

"How?" she asks.

"I'm not sure yet . . . I'll figure it out and I'll let you know . . . just keep your phone close, okay?" I look to Mary Claire, who gives me a nod, and then I end the call.

"Oh my," Mary Claire says as we approach Westhaven's gate. "Well, this isn't good."

Up ahead, pulling into the gated driveway, is Wells in his unmistakable Daytona gray Audi coupe.

I check the time on my phone. "He isn't supposed to be home for another three hours."

"Maybe that's why he was calling you a little bit ago."

"What do we do now?" I nibble my thumbnail and ignore the prickle of sweat on the back of my neck. After everything that's transpired over the past half hour, it's going to be impossible pretending everything's fine.

Mary Claire pulls into the gate. I step out and enter the code before climbing back into the passenger seat.

"We act natural," she says as we drive forward. "We had lunch, we wanted to lounge by the pool this afternoon, we know *nothing*."

35

JADE

"Before we go inside, take this." Mary Claire digs into her center console and pulls out a prepaid debit card. "I keep this on hand for when I forget my wallet. It happens from time to time. But there's enough on there to get you at least three or four nights at a decent hotel. That'll buy us some time to figure out your next move."

"How am I supposed to leave if my car is at the restaurant."

"Uber . . . Lyft . . . phone a friend? Time to think outside the box." She lifts a single finger in the air. "Before I forget, let me message my private investigator. What's the name of the restaurant we just ate at?"

"Michel's on the Bay," I say.

"And your plate number?"

I rattle off the numbers and letters, make and model, and she taps everything into her phone.

"I'm going to have him do a sweep of your car and make sure there are no tracking devices or any fun little surprises waiting for you when you get it back," she says.

"You never gave me Cathleen's number," I tell her.

"That's right." She pulls up her contacts and AirDrops me the number of Cathleen Purcell.

A moment later, Mary Claire parks her Mercedes behind Wells's coupe, and we head in through the side door, using my fingerprint on the lock.

"Hey, hey." I pretend to be pleasantly surprised when I find Wells in his study. "What are you doing home so early?"

He peers up over his laptop screen before frowning. "I forgot some things at home, figured I'd just work the rest of the afternoon remotely."

"Mary Claire's with me . . . we were going to lay by the pool this afternoon," I say. "I think she's ordering drinks right now from Margot in the kitchen."

Wells checks his watch, but if he's wondering why we're drinking so early in the day, he keeps his question to himself.

"We had a nice lunch," I say, remembering Mary Claire's advice to act natural. "Went to this new place on La Playa."

"Mm-hmm, that's nice," he says, though he isn't really listening.

Leaning against the doorjamb, I watch my husband—or rather, my soon-to-be-ex-husband, taking in his devilishly handsome face one last time, before it all goes up in flames (as it should).

"You're staring," he says. "Why are you staring?"

"Can't a girl admire a work of art?" I tease him with something the old me would have said, before she knew of his sociopathic ways.

How I didn't see any of this sooner is beyond me. He has all the classic telltale signs. He's antisocial, has no regard for right or wrong, and couldn't care less about anyone's feelings besides his own.

Heading upstairs, I change into something better suited for poolside lounging, but not before disappearing into the corner of Viviette's closet and making a phone call.

With my phone in my trembling hand, I pull up the contact information for Cathleen Purcell and press the green button.

The phone rings once . . . twice . . . three times . . .

I'm certain it'll go to voicemail, when suddenly a woman answers.

"Hello?" she says.

"Hi, yes," I keep my voice down, hardly above a whisper. "Is this Cathleen Purcell? Sylvie's mother?"

She doesn't answer back, not right away.

"Yes, this is she. Whom may I ask is calling?" she asks.

"My name is Jade Westmore," I say. "I'm married to Wells Westmore."

"Is this some kind of joke?"

"Pardon me?"

"My daughter is married to Wells. You're trying to tell me you're married to him, too? Or wait, did she get divorced? Because if she did, I wouldn't know. She quit talking to me about three years ago."

"She was in an accident three years ago," I say. Quickly adding, "She's alive, but she's living in the guesthouse at Westhaven."

"My daughter was in an accident? Is this your idea of a joke? You don't think my own son-in-law would've maybe mentioned that to me? I know we weren't on speaking terms, but my God . . ."

"Your son-in-law divorced her, married me, and he told me you died shortly after her accident. I didn't know you were alive until Mary Claire called you today."

Cathleen doesn't speak.

"That's the real reason she called you," I say, "to prove you were still living. She wasn't calling about cats."

Pulling my phone from my ear, I check to make sure she hasn't hung up.

She's still there.

"I want to talk to my daughter," she says. "Now."

"I'm going to do everything in my power to make that happen," I say, now that I know for sure that Mary Claire was being truthful. "Just, whatever you do, don't call Wells, don't breathe a word of any of this to him, okay?"

"He's kept me from my daughter for three years and I'm not supposed to give him a piece of my mind?"

"Not yet," I say. "You'll get your day, but for now, I need you to be patient. Save my number. I'll be in touch soon."

Ending the call, I change into a swimsuit and silk sarong, accessorize it with a wide-brimmed hat and a brave face, and head out to the pool to meet Mary Claire to strategize.

"You're doing great," she says under her breath. "We've got this."

36

JADE

"I need to tell you something, but you have to promise you'll stay calm," I tell Sylvie that night.

Wells took a phone call after dinner, and I took the opportunity to visit my silent predecessor.

"We're going to get you out of here," I say.

Her brows meet, and her lips move, but nothing comes out. It's clear she has strong feelings on this matter, but I've no doubt they'll change once she hears the truth.

"The reason Olly attacked you that night," I whisper, "is because Wells paid him to."

Her eyes narrow and her hands clench into two fists. I can't imagine the torment of being full of emotion with no way to let it out.

"Wells *wanted* to scare you," I say. "Olly has all the text messages to prove it. Not only that, but Mary Claire adored you. She was being awful to you on purpose, to try to push you out of the marriage."

She blinks twice, as if she disagrees.

"I know, I know." I throw my hands up. "I know how it sounds, and I know this is a lot to take in, but you have to trust me on this."

She blinks again, and again, and again, as if she's disagreeing, and I get it. She's confused. She doesn't know what to believe. She's me mere hours ago, wild eyed and disbelieving.

"I spoke to your mother today," I say, checking to make sure the nurse is still out of earshot. "She had no idea anything had happened to you. She thought you were mad at her. Wells convinced her you didn't want to speak to her. Apparently you two had a falling out shortly before you got hurt. Wells led her to believe your silence was related to that. Anyway, she can't wait to see you. I'm taking you to her house tomorrow."

Sylvie's eyes begin to water, and I can only hope these are happy tears.

"Excuse me, Mrs. Westmore?" The nurse—one I've not seen until tonight—pokes her head into the kitchen where we're seated. "Can I talk to you for a minute?"

"I'll be right back," I tell Sylvie before following the nurse to the hall. "What's going on?"

"I was changing Sylvie's pillowcases, and I found these." She uncurls her palm to reveal an assortment of pills, maybe a dozen or so of them. "And this is on top of the ones I found under her sofa cushions. And the bottles I found at the bottom of her trash can. I don't think she's been taking all of her meds . . ."

Steeling myself, I don't react. But it's clear to see she's been tapering off her meds and while I'm no doctor, I have a hunch it has something to do with her ability to communicate again.

"Thank you for letting me know," I say. Thinking fast, I add, "She actually has an appointment in the morning, so I'll mention it to her doctor then."

"Should I mention it to Mr. Westmore?" she asks.

"No, no. I'll talk to him about it," I say before leaning in and lowering my voice, "I don't want to get any of the nurses or the agency in trouble for not monitoring her medications closer."

I'm far from a master manipulator and seldom can I think this quickly on my feet, but I'm positive Mary Claire would be proud of me in this moment.

The nurse's eyes widen and she nods. "Yes, thank you. I appreciate that."

Returning to the kitchen, I sit across from Sylvie.

"You've been overmedicated for years . . . haven't you?" I ask.

She blinks once.

"He kept you silent on purpose." It's more of a statement than a question. "My God."

She doesn't blink. But she doesn't know the full story, the full scope of how deep this goes.

But she'll know.

Soon she'll know everything.

I tell Sylvie to get some good rest tonight, that I'll be taking her to the doctor in the morning, and then I linger outside before heading back to the main house so I can call Mary Claire.

"Sylvie's been scaling back on her meds—that's why she's been able to communicate with me," I say when she answers.

"Wells was overmedicating her. Of course. It makes perfect sense now," she says. "I had my suspicions over the years, but I was never allowed anywhere near her. All I knew was what he wanted me to know—that she was incapable of speaking ever again."

"We have to get her out of here. Who knows what he'll do to her when I'm gone. I'm the only advocate she has, the only one here who knows what's really going on."

"Take her with you tomorrow," she says.

"That's the plan. Wells leaves for work around seven thirty. I'll check his calendar and make sure we leave when he's in a meeting. I already told the nurse Sylvie has an appointment in the morning and I'm the one taking her."

"Look at you, thinking outside the box." A hint of a proud smile resides in her voice. "Keep me posted and let me know if you need anything between now and then."

I end the call with Mary Claire and call Portia, telling her to gather all the evidence she can, as soon as possible. To make copies of everything. To hire an attorney for Olly. And to be prepared for whatever comes next.

Tomorrow's the day.

37

JADE

I can't sleep next to him tonight—at least not longer than I have to.

I hide out in Viviette's room under the guise of a late-night writing session. Poring over all of her belongings, I take a moment to stand in awe of her legacy one final time. As soon as I leave Wells, he's going to pull the plug on the book. All of my work will have been for nothing and I'll have to pay back my advance, but if it means getting out of a potentially lethal marriage and saving Sylvie along the way, it'll be worth it.

There will be other books.

And there's no shortage of iconic women to write about, though odds are I'll never again have the chance to marry into their families.

Snapping on a pair of nitrile gloves, I page through the last of Viviette's diaries: number thirty. Most of the entries are from her final year, her handwriting growing shakier and harder to read by the page. A good portion of them are impossible to read without squinting and guessing at half of the words.

Placing it aside, I carefully make my way around her room, quietly pulling out dresser drawers and lifting the corners of her mattress to check for any tucked away notebooks. Back in my younger years, when my sister first realized I was reading her diary, she'd move it around the room, getting more creative each time. Eventually she graduated from stuffing it in shoeboxes to placing fake book jackets on it to taping it underneath her nightstand.

With nothing but time on my hands and a backlog of pent-up, nervous energy, I check every square inch of Viviette's room, going so far as to check behind framed photos on the wall as well as inching my body beneath her bed to check the frame.

It isn't until I'm standing in the center of her closet, beneath her glimmering chandelier, that I catch a glimpse of something strange reflecting off the mirror. Nestled under a stack of sweaters is an out-of-place hatbox, haphazardly covered by folds of wool and cashmere. Carefully sliding it out, I flip up the lid and gasp.

Six journals—numbers twenty-four through twenty-nine—are stacked inside the box.

Carrying them to her desk, I adjust my gloves and page through the first one. Then the second. The third. Fourth. Fifth. And lastly, the sixth.

Today I'm quite worried about Wells. While I've always been aware of his troubling tendencies to grow hyper-attached to various love interests, he came home from college this weekend and informed me that his lovely girlfriend, Layla, jumped off a bridge in downtown LA. She survived—thank goodness. Apparently someone spotted her and the fire department came with some sort of contraption to catch her. But the most perturbing part about this, is it isn't the first time one of his girlfriends has attempted to take her own life. It isn't the second time either.

I'm sensing a pattern.

And I'm beside myself with worry.

To be honest, I'm not sure what to make of it.

I know what I want to believe. And I also know that he is his mother's child and his mother is my child and we have a tendency toward extreme ways in every facet of our lives.

I close the sixth journal and place everything back into the hatbox before placing it exactly the way I found it.

With shaking hands and a breath that rattles in my chest, I flick off the lamp at Viviette's desk, collect my laptop and notebook, and head to our room. While I'd much prefer to sleep anywhere else tonight, I have to keep up appearances or he'll know something is off.

Hell, maybe he already knows.

I crawl under the covers a few minutes later, and while he's half asleep, he still senses me the instant I settle in. Sliding me into his arms, he holds me close, his breath hot on top of my head. Despite his delicate hold around me, my body tenses as if it's being held in a vice grip.

I listen to the steady thrum of his heart in his chest, and I breathe in his intoxicating scent, silently mourning the life I was so certain we were going to have together. I should've known fairy tales only exist in fiction books and imaginations.

None of this was real, but I'm grateful to have learned this early on and not when it's too late.

It dawns on me now, as I lie in this warm soft bed, in Wells's tender embrace, that if it weren't for Sylvie and all that has transpired these past two weeks, I never would've made it out of this marriage alive.

38

JADE

I start packing the instant he leaves, though I can't make it obvious. He has cameras all over the house, cameras that never made me think twice until yesterday.

I place my things in laundry baskets, carrying them up and down the stairs on the camera, though I'm placing them by the side door, loading them into my trunk every few trips.

I unplugged the camera that points to that section of the driveway. Wells will likely get a notification on his app that a device went offline, but before he has a chance to check into it, we'll be long gone, and by the time he realizes what happened, the police will be reading him his Miranda rights.

My only regret is that I won't be there to see it in person.

No, that isn't true.

I have other regrets . . . regrets I don't have time to fixate on right now because I need to focus on getting us out of here.

When I'm finished throwing the last of my things into my car, I head to the guesthouse and get Sylvie from the nurse. She's dressed in ordinary clothes today. No nightshirts or dressing gowns. Just blue jeans, a gray T-shirt, and crisp white Converse sneakers that look like they've been worn twice their whole life. Her mousy hair is slicked back into a tight, unflattering ponytail that pulls her facial features taut. But there's a beautiful sort of courage emanating from her today, and that's all that matters.

I load her into the passenger side and enter her mother's address into the GPS, but before we leave, we take one last look at Westhaven.

I imagine our thoughts are more alike than they are different.

In silence, we say goodbye to a place that once held our respective hopes and dreams, only to become our living nightmares.

"Ready to see your mom?" I ask her as we coast down the Westhaven driveway for the last time.

Tears fill her eyes, which are a little brighter than they were the last time I saw them, and she blinks once.

A moment later, I'm backing out into the street. Checking the rearview, I shift into drive. It's then that I notice a black SUV parked in the street. His headlights flick on and he pulls out of his parking spot.

By the time I make it to the next stop sign, he's behind me—a man in a baseball cap.

I glance at Sylvie from my periphery, watching her sit there with her hands limp in her lap, the seatbelt holding her tight, and her eyes trained on the dash. She's unaffected, unaware.

I make a left at the next intersection.

The SUV makes a left.

The GPS instructs me to turn right at the next light, but I make another left to see if he follows.

He does.

Jaw clenched, I reach for my phone to call Mary Claire—only I can't call her because Wells is calling me.

He was supposed to be in a meeting . . .

I made sure of that.

I must have checked his calendar a dozen times between yesterday and this morning.

Either way, I answer because I have to know what he knows, and I have to play dumb in case he's onto me.

"Hey," I answer, injecting a smile into my tone. "What's up?"

"What are you doing?" he asks, though the cadence of his tone is far from friendly or casual. It's more along the lines of accusatory.

"What do you mean?"

"You're in your car," he says. "I can hear the road noise. You going somewhere?"

My heart races and my palms grow damp against my leather steering wheel. I wipe them against the tops of my thighs before checking my rearview again.

I'm still being tailed.

"Just running some errands," I say.

"With Sylvie?" he asks.

He knows.

"Care to explain what's really going on?" he asks. "Her nurse said you were taking her to the doctor, but I just took her in a few weeks ago. She's not due for a follow-up for another two months."

"I thought we could get a second opinion," I say. It's not a lie. I'm picking up Cathleen and then we're taking Sylvie to Cedars-Sinai, where she can get a full evaluation, a barrage of tests, and they can start tapering her off of all of her medications. It's going to be a process, but Mary Claire put us in touch with a couple of doctors there who are aware of the situation and more than willing to step in.

"For what?" he asks.

I make another left.

The SUV stays straight.

Exhaling, I almost decide to pull over to collect myself, but there's no time for that. We're en route to Cathleen's. Until then, Sylvie's not safe. And until Wells is arrested, neither am I.

"I'll fill you in on everything later," I say, knowing full well he won't be hearing any of this from me.

"Jade, this is not okay," he says. "You don't have permission to take her anywhere. This isn't your place. It's—"

I end the call.

I have nothing more to say to the man whose core purpose in life is to drive women to the brink of insanity so he doesn't have to be alone.

He doesn't deserve an explanation.

He knows damn well what he's done.

He calls again, and I press the red button on my phone. I've never rejected a call from Wells in my life and I'm sure it'll only upset him even more, but I have nothing more to say to him.

Wells calls a third time.

And a fourth.

By the time he calls a fifth time, I wait until I'm stopped at a long light before blocking his number. A strange sensation falls over me when I'm done, a cocktail of sadness and melancholy with a side of denial.

While I never thought we'd be together forever—marriages seldom last that long in this day and age—I never thought we'd go out like this.

The GPS leads me to the freeway a moment later and a black SUV rockets past me, stealing the wind from my lungs for a moment.

I call Mary Claire and let her know we're halfway to Cathleen's, and then I call Cathleen to tell her the same.

"Tell her I can't wait to see her again," Cathleen says over the speakers in my car. "I've missed her so much."

I turn to Sylvie, who turns to me. She blinks once. And then she reaches her hand out, placing it over mine.

"Think it's safe to say the feeling's mutual," I tell Cathleen.

The side of Sylvie's mouth lifts into some semblance of a smile. There's nothing infectious or contagious about it like in her wedding photos. She certainly isn't lit from within. But there's a spark of something in her eyes that wasn't there before.

Wells may have stolen her light.

But I'm going to make damn sure she gets it back.

39

JADE

"Mr. Westmore is here," Sylvie's hospital nurse says.

He'd called Mary Claire two hours ago, casually pretending to be looking for me. She feigned ignorance, claiming she was at some spa retreat in Sonoma. Portia's keeping an eye on the house, watching for any police cars to pull up. So far there's been nothing, which means there are more important matters for the detectives to tend to than an old, closed assault case.

Either way, he can't come near her.

I won't allow it.

"He can't be in here," I tell her.

She exhales, her face colored with frustration, but she throws her hands up. "He says he's her power of attorney, and he brought all the forms."

"He's also been abusing her," I say. "And restricting her communication with her family. It's a police matter."

"Did you file a report?" she asks.

"Not yet," I say. Perhaps we should've gone straight to the police after leaving Westhaven, but I wanted to get her to her mother and then to a hospital. I figured sooner or later the police would come to us.

"I can't restrict him from her without a police report," she says. "As it stands now, he has full power of attorney, and I have to let him in. Hospital policy."

Cathleen and I exchange looks.

"No," Cathleen says, rising from her seat next to her daughter's bed. "That man is a monster. He'll never set foot near my daughter again. I'll make sure of that."

The nurse closes her eyes, gathers her composure, and says, "He wants the two of you out of Sylvie's room."

"Absolutely not," Cathleen says, grinding her heeled foot into the linoleum tile floor. "He'll have to drag me out of here kicking and screaming."

"Sylvie." Wells rushes in behind the nurse.

He pushes past us and steals the chair Cathleen was occupying a moment ago.

The heart monitor connected to Sylvie's finger beeps in quick succession when he slides his hand over hers. Her vacant stare searches the room before landing on Cathleen. She can't look at him. Or she won't. Either way, she's uncomfortable.

"He's stressing her out," Cathleen says. "Get him out of here."

Wells ignores her, leaning closer to Sylvie.

"My God, you must be terrified," he tells her, sweeping a strand of hair from her forehead. She flinches. "I called every hospital and medical center in the city until I found you. I'm going to get you home where you belong."

"She's been fully admitted," the nurse says. "You'd be taking her against medical advice."

"Admitted for *what*?" His face is contorted as he shoots her a chilling glare. "There's nothing wrong with her."

"Nothing wrong with her?" I scoff. "You've been overmedicating her for years. You're the reason she hasn't been able to communicate. We're getting her detoxed and rehabilitated. She's not leaving until she gets her life back—the life you stole when you hired Olly to attack her that night."

Rising slowly, he turns to me, scraping his hand along his sharp jawline.

If looks could kill, I'd be a goner right now.

"I don't know what you *think* you know." He speaks between gritted teeth, though the slight tremor in his voice tells me he's bluffing. "But you're dead wrong."

He's on a sinking ship, and he knows it.

It's officially the beginning of the end for Wells Westmore.

My phone buzzes with a text from Mary Claire.

MARY CLAIRE: Just talked to Portia. The police are still looking for him. He wasn't at the office and he's not home.

ME: Yeah . . . I know. He's here. At the hospital. In her room. I'm looking at him.

MARY CLAIRE: Keep him there as long as you can. I'll send them that way.

ME: I'll try . . .

"Cathleen, can I have a word with you in the hall please?" I ask.

She furrows her brow. "I'm not leaving Sylvie."

"It'll only take a moment," I say.

"What are you trying to pull now?" Wells asks in a tone he's never used with me before. I'm no longer his wife—I'm his enemy. I'm the one about to take him down and he knows it. If he thought he had a snowball's chance in hell at convincing me I'm wrong, he'd be trying right now, but he isn't. He's basking in his own denial, wearing the mask he wears to fool the rest of the world.

"I'm not leaving my daughter," Cathleen reiterates.

"Assuming whatever you need to discuss concerns Sylvie, anything you have to say to Cathleen, you can say in front of me," Wells says. "I have the final say-so regarding her care."

Not for much longer . . .

I check the time. It's only been two minutes since Mary Claire texted me, which means the police are likely a ways away.

"I need to take Sylvie to level four for some more tests," the nurse says as she wheels a wheelchair up to the bed. "We'll be back in about half an hour."

"You're not taking her anywhere," Wells says. "I want to talk to her doctor before you do anything—her actual doctor, not some hospitalist who's known her for all of five minutes."

Cathleen and the nurse ignore him, working to help Sylvie into the wheelchair as Wells continues to run his mouth. I've never seen him so desperate, so worked up. His hands are in his hair and his face is growing redder by the second.

He's the portrait of a man losing all control.

The nurse wheels Sylvie out of the room, and Cathleen follows. She's not going to let her daughter out of her sight, and I can't blame her.

For now, it's just the two of us, and I swear the room has dropped ten degrees.

"You have no idea what you've just done," he says, his chin tucked down and his voice low and soft. "You have no idea what you're throwing away . . . and for what? For some woman who never would've given you the time of day in her former life."

"Maybe," I say. "But I guess we'll never know."

"You want to know why I chose you, Jade? Why I picked you out of everyone I could've chosen?"

"Not really." I cross my arms.

"Because you're low-hanging fruit," he says. "You were starstruck when we met. And I knew I could give you something you'd never have with anyone else. I made you happy, Jade. Truly happy."

"You did," I say. "But none of it was real. It was all an act. You never loved me. None of this was about love for you. It was about not being alone. That's why you picked me. You thought you were better than me, smarter than me, that I'd never see through any of it. But you thought wrong. You *picked* the wrong piece of low-hanging fruit, Wells."

An incredulous smirk fills his face and for the first time, his good looks turn from charming to downright devilish.

He's about to say something to me when he stops. His mouth flattens and his attention skims past my shoulder, toward the doorway.

Turning, I find two uniformed security guards entering.

"Oh, good, you came," he says. "I'd like this woman escorted off the premises immediately. She's not allowed to be near Sylvie Westmore."

The men ignore Wells, stride past me, and go directly to him.

"Sir, we're going to need you to come with us," one of them says.

Wells laughs.

Laughs.

Like this is funny to him.

"I'm not going anywhere. I'm waiting here for my ex-wife to get back," he says. "And then I'm taking her home."

"LAPD is en route now," the man says. "They called us and asked that we assist in apprehending you until they get here."

"Apprehending me? For what?" The wicked smile on his face melts.

"They'll talk to you about that when they get here," the guard on the left says.

The guard on the right slips his hand around Wells's elbow, but Wells jerks it away.

"Don't touch me," he says, smoothing the crisp lapels of his suit coat.

"Willingly come with us and I won't have to," the guard replies, his hand moving to the shiny set of handcuffs hanging from his belt.

"This is ridiculous," Wells spews, shooting daggers my way as he heads for the door. "You'll be hearing from my divorce attorney tomorrow."

"I'll be ready to sign on the dotted line," I say as they show him out.

The last thing I see is the back of his head, his sandy hair combed perfectly without a strand out of place and his designer suit hugging his broad shoulders.

I wish I could remember him like that—perfect.

Instead, every time I think of Wells Westmore from here on out, I'm going to think of this moment, of his fall from grace, and of his uncanny ability to behave like a normal person when all eyes are on him and behave like a monster when he thinks no one's looking.

Taking a seat, I text Portia and Mary Claire with an update.

And then I sit in awe, digesting the events of the past twenty-four hours as they play on a surreal loop in my head.

To think, I could have been his next victim . . .

Steering my thoughts from turning too dark, I remind myself of one thing and one thing only: Wells Westmore will never silence another woman again.

Epilogue

SYLVIE

One Year Later

"Sylvie? Jade's here to see you." My mother knocks on my door before stepping aside.

"Jade, hi." I push myself up from my desk chair and make my way across my bedroom.

A year ago, making this kind of trek would have felt like running a marathon. With the nauseating cocktail of prescription medications streaming through my system, nothing was functioning the way it was supposed to. I was constantly fatigued, unable to form coherent sentences, and dealing with uncontrolled fits of rage alternating with periods where I'd sleep for what felt like forever. I'm told I was sedated during those periods, though my memory from that time is still cloudy.

It's probably for the best.

I know now that my ex-husband, Wells, was working with a doctor to keep me incapacitated. And if it weren't for Jade, and Mary Claire, I would still be incapacitated, existing in a perpetual zombielike state and planted in front of a TV, waiting for Wells's sparse visits where he would look at me with both awe and disgust—like a sideshow attraction kept in a cage for sick amusement.

I try not to think about that time, though it haunts me every day.

My therapist says I'll forever be a work in progress, but all that matters is I'm making progress.

"I brought you something." Jade places a paperback on my lap, and I flip the cover over to find an advance copy of *The Women of Westmore*. The cover is a brilliant royal blue and in the center of it all is an image of the same gold, heart-shaped locket we all have.

Flipping through the first few pages, I stop when I find the dedication.

To Sylvie Purcell, the first Mrs. Westmore.

Nothing more, nothing less, and yet somehow, enough said.

After Wells was arrested for conspiracy to commit murder, he was immediately booked. The judge, after hearing the case, denied his bail, and he has sat there waiting for his trial ever since. In the meantime, he gave Mary Claire power of attorney so she could help manage his funds. As far as we know, he still has no idea Mary Claire was the one who helped shed light on his misdeeds. She's also the one who authorized the biography and worked tirelessly with Jade to see it to completion.

"How's Portia doing?" I ask. Last I heard, she and Lee had finally gone their separate ways. I can't say that I'm surprised nor disappointed. She deserved better than him.

"Great. Just settled into the new place with Lily," Jade says. "I think it's going to be good for her, being on her own. She doesn't realize how strong she is, you know?"

"Do any of us?"

Jade laughs. "Fair point."

"How's Olly?" After everything went down last year, the judge gave Olly six months of probation and one hundred hours of community service. A few local citizens were upset, calling it a slap on the wrist—until they learned the full story.

The two of us have sat down as well, and he explained to me that he never meant to hurt me that night, that Wells simply wanted him to scare me. But I put up such a good fight that he panicked and threw me into the water, where I hit my head on the edge of the pool. He found my necklace lying on the concrete and grabbed it on his way out. He claims he doesn't know why he took it, just that his mind was blank and he was simply going through the motions.

Sometimes I think had he not kept that locket and had Jade not found it that fateful day, none of this would have happened. Or perhaps it would have played out differently. I don't like to think about it if I don't have to. It's better to focus on the present and the future rather than wallow in the unchangeable past.

I don't live there anymore.

"He's doing well," Jade says. "Portia has him in this independent living apartment with three other young men his age, and they're all learning basic life skills. It was hard for her, to let him spread his wings like that, but I think she's at peace with the decision now that she sees how much he's thriving."

"She's a good mom."

"The best."

"So tell me about this upcoming book tour," I say as I fan through her book. I stop when I get to the photo sections, lingering on all the beautiful images of Viviette through the years. I've never been much of a reader, if only because sitting still with my own thoughts was a prison sentence in my twenties and my thirties were mostly lived in servitude to Wells.

Jade rattles off all the stops she's most excited about as well as some of the fun activities they have planned during their downtime. A concert in Saint Paul. A comedy show in Portland. A lighthouse in Chesapeake Bay. A walking ghost tour in Savannah. A Victorian Airbnb in New Orleans. Mary Claire is accompanying her on a few of her stops, so readers will get a chance to meet Viviette's daughter and get an autograph as well.

I wish I were able to go, but first things first.

I need to be able to function outside of my mother's home, without a daily schedule of rigorous occupational, speech, and physical therapy.

The medications I was on really did a number on me, and it didn't help that I was spending most of my days in bed or in a recliner, my muscles virtually wasting away by the minute.

The first day I met her—Jade . . . the new Mrs. Westmore—I knew I had to warn her. I knew Olly had assaulted me and I knew Wells had a controlling side, but I didn't know how to get her attention. It took all the strength I had to scribble that word on that torn slip of paper, and while I wasn't sure how it would be interpreted, I knew it could be my only chance at getting her attention.

After that, I started hiding pills, flushing them, discarding them . . . anything I could do to avoid swallowing them. Each day, my thoughts became a little more lucid. My coordination began to return. The tranquilized sensation that weighed through my bones seemed to dissipate by the hour.

I didn't want to believe Wells was intentionally overmedicating me, but it turns out that was exactly what he was doing. Looking back, it was plain as day—I just didn't have the coherence to comprehend it at the time.

"I hate to cut this short, but my speech therapist is going to be here any minute," I say after an hour into our visit.

"Walk me out?" Jade asks, knowing how much it means to me to be able to do something most people take for granted.

"It was good seeing you." While I speak a little slower these days and occasionally I trip over my own tongue and jumble my words together, my speech is coming back to me, day by day, word by word.

An ex once told me there was power in silence.

After three years of quietude, I couldn't disagree more.

My power is in my voice, and that's something Wells can never take away from me again.

About the Author

Photo © 2024 Jill Austin Photography

Minka Kent is the *Washington Post* and *Wall Street Journal* bestselling author of *After Dark, The Watcher Girl, When I Was You, The Stillwater Girls, The Thinnest Air, The Perfect Roommate, The Memory Watcher, Unmissing, The Silent Woman, Gone Again, People Like Them, After Dark,* and *Imaginary Strangers.* Her work has been featured in *People* magazine and the *New York Post* as well as optioned for film and TV. Minka also writes contemporary romance as *Wall Street Journal* and #1 Amazon Charts bestselling author Winter Renshaw. She is a graduate of Iowa State University and resides in Iowa with her three children. For more information, visit http://minkakent.com.